I0660758

Mrs. Alfred Cock

The Life of Madame de Longueville

Anne-Geneviève de Bourbon

Mrs. Alfred Cock

The Life of Madame de Longueville
Anne-Geneviève de Bourbon

ISBN/EAN: 9783337333676

Printed in Europe, USA, Canada, Australia, Japan

Cover: Foto ©Raphael Reischuk / pixelio.de

More available books at **www.hansebooks.com**

THE LIFE

OF

MADAME DE LONGUEVILLE

(ANNE-GENEVIÈVE DE BOURBON)

BY

MRS ALFRED COCK

WITH A PORTRAIT

LONDON

SMITH, ELDER, & CO., 15 WATERLOO PLACE

1899

[All rights reserved]

CONTENTS

MADAME DE LONGUEVILLE

INTRODUCTION

Few women in history have come down to us with such a living personality as Madame de Longueville. The excellent portraits of her which have been preserved, the admiring and affectionate descriptions to be found in the letters of her numerous friends, in the great memoirs of the period, and in contemporary fiction, her own correspondence and written confession, for religious purposes, and last, not least, the patient researches into her life and biographical tributes to her memory of the brilliant philosopher who styled himself her posthumous lover, have brought her wonderfully near to us. All these things

B

enable us to feel her personal charm and to love her, in spite of the indiscretions of one portion of her private life and the grave and more far-reaching political mistakes for which she herself thought twenty-five years of the severest penance and self-humiliation but an insufficient atonement.

Victor Cousin died before he had completed the series of social and biographical studies of remarkable seventeenth-century Frenchwomen, of which the Duchesse de Longueville is the central and, in every sense, the greatest figure. Although it is difficult to find among the memoirs and correspondences of her time a book or a manuscript in which the sister of the great Prince de Condé and cousin of Louis XIV. is not referred to, the only life of her ever written is an eighteenth-century publication of very little merit, either literary or biographical, not being the work either of an eyewitness or of an historian familiar with the methods of modern research.

Therefore it has seemed worth while to put together the main facts of her life as they can

now be known, and to endeavour to glean from
so many witnesses the secret of the powerful
influence and the irresistible fascination of one
of the most delightful women of all times and
countries.

CHAPTER I

EARLY YOUTH AND MARRIAGE—THE HÔTEL DE
RAMBOUILLET—THE CONGRESS OF MÜNSTER

THE life of Anne Geneviève de Bourbon is a romance from the very outset. She was born on August 28, 1619, in the dungeon of Vincennes where her father, Henri II. de Bourbon, third Prince of Condé and 'first Prince of the Blood,' was a prisoner, and where, for two years, her beautiful mother, Charlotte Marguerite de Montmorency, granddaughter of the great Constable of France, had voluntarily shut herself up with him.

Contemporary opinion seems to have been unanimous in considering her one of the loveliest women of her time, and when she first appeared at Court, at the age of fifteen, in 1609, Henri IV. fell in love with her. Having prevented her union with the man to whom her hand had been promised, he married her to his cousin, the Prince de Condé,[1] from whom he expected a subserviency which the latter was not disposed to show. Good King Henri's heart remained to the end as susceptible as it had always been, and the young Princess was destined to be his last passion. The unforeseen obstacle only increased it, and at last 'Monsieur le Prince' saw no other way out of the difficulty than to carry off his wife and fly to Brussels, where she was admired by, among others, Cardinal Bentivoglio, who has left an enthusiastic description of her.[2] Here they remained until the assassination of the King in 1610.

The Princes of Condé were descended from Robert le Fort (866), the common ancestor of the whole family of Bourbon, through the youngest son of St. Louis, Robert of France, Count of Clermont. The latter inherited, through his wife Beatrix, a barony, which was afterwards erected into a duchy in favour of his son

---

[1] Contrat de mariage de M. le Prince de Condé avec Charlotte Marguerite de Montmorency, 1600. Ancien fonds 4663, fol. 171 (*Bibliothèque Nationale*).

[2] Cardinal Bentivoglio, *Relazioni*.

Louis, and gave the name of Bourbon to his posterity. As each 'son of France' took a separate title, his individual descendants assumed the name of the head of their house, so that all the members of a younger branch of the royal family called themselves de Valois, d'Artois, or whatever was the title of their head. When Henri IV. came to the throne the name of Bourbon was used only by the Condés and the Montpensiers, who had branched off before the death of Henri III. The kings who succeeded and were descended from Henri IV. were styled 'de France,' but, in accordance with the rule in question, the descendants of the second son of Louis XIII. called themselves d'Orléans, from the title borne by their grandfather.

The third Prince de Condé was the grandson of the late King's first cousin, Louis I. de Bourbon, the first Prince, and, barring his two sons, his nearest relation. It is, therefore, not impossible that, at the instigation of the Spanish authorities in the Netherlands, he may have contemplated having himself placed on the throne. At any rate, he allowed himself to be received with almost royal honours by the Princes of Lorraine and Sully, and made a triumphal entry into Paris.

This, together with various other incidents, so alarmed the Queen-Regent, Marie de Médicis, that she caused Condé to be arrested and incarcerated in the Bastille, where he remained a whole year. After the Queen's disgrace the Ministers transferred their prisoner to Vincennes, and there his young wife continued to share, with the greatest fortitude, the fate of a husband for whom she had never cared.

They had two sons, born in prison, who died almost immediately. Three months after the birth of Anne Geneviève Monsieur le Prince recovered his liberty, and the young King Louis XIII. took him back into favour. 'Madame la Princesse,' with her little daughter, returned to the Hôtel de Condé in Paris, where she became at once the centre of the most brilliant society. Here were born, in 1621, the greatest military genius of his century, Louis de Bourbon, Duc d'Enghien, who became 'le Grand Condé,'

and, in 1629, Armand, Prince de Conti, both of
whom, in different ways, were through life, with
short intervals of estrangement, the devoted
knights and followers of their fascinating
sister.

During their childhood and early youth
they hardly ever met. Their father, a remarkable though by no means a lovable character,
intellectually far in advance of his time, entertained views upon education which are worthy
of our own.

He was determined that neither of his two
sons should receive the amateurish and exceptional teaching then considered fit for royal
princes. The younger, on account of his
delicate health, was at first destined for the
Church, although he eventually became a
soldier. His general studies at the Jesuits'
College at Clermont, and afterwards his theological training at Bourges, were of the
thoroughest and most solid kind, and he was not
allowed to appear in society until 1647.

The Duc d'Enghien, who, as the eldest,
was to continue the greatness of the House of

Condé, was sent to the Jesuits' College at
Bourges, where his father, then Governor of
the province of Berri and, afterwards, of
Burgundy, was frequently in residence. Here,
under the Prince's most careful supervision, he
went through that astonishing intellectual
training which, more even than his personal
bravery, helped to make him the greatest general
of his time, and so scientific and modern in his
methods of warfare that one is more inclined
to compare him to Napoleon I. than to establish
parallels between his warlike achievements
and those of any of his predecessors or contemporaries. History, philosophy, and mathe-
matics were the principal features of the
educational programme. The physical training was perfect, and the King's young cousin
shared the discipline common to all. The
same system was continued when he entered
Benjamin's celebrated 'Academy.' It was
there the Duc d'Enghien began to be surrounded by that brilliant troop of young men
who afterwards formed a kind of general staff
which gravitated round him, sharing in his

labours and his glory, and for whose reputation and advancement he was always more solicitous than for his own.

It is scarcely necessary to recall that at the age of twenty-two he had already distinguished himself in the field, in such a manner that after the death of Richelieu, King Louis XIII., on his deathbed, appointed him Generalissimo of the French army sent to defend the frontier against the Spaniards.

The education of his sister was of necessity a totally different one. In fact, as her biographer, Villefore, quaintly puts it,[1] those in charge of it very soon discovered there was nothing for them to do.

Mademoiselle de Bourbon, as she was styled, possessed by common consent every gift of mind as well as of body. From her earliest youth till the end of her life, when she was inclined to look upon it as a sinful craving, she loved nothing so much as the pleasures of the intellect. From the very first she lived

---

[1] *La Véritable Vie d'Anne Geneviève de Bourbon, Duchesse de Longueville*, par Bourgoing de Villefore (Amsterdam, 1739).

in an atmosphere of culture. Her girlhood corresponded to the palmy days of the Hôtel de Rambouillet, where her mother was as well qualified to shine as everywhere else. She imbibed literary tastes at an age when girls nowadays are in the nursery. Real life began years earlier than it does in our time. But a certain aristocratic indolence and languor, of which all her contemporaries speak as of an additional charm, prevented her from ever exerting her mind in any way. In after-life, when her literary judgments had come to be looked upon as authoritative, her letters were constantly incorrect in grammar and style, and her spelling remained that of the majority of very great ladies of her time. Her moral training, on the other hand, left nothing to be desired. In addition to the influence of her mother, a truly refined and noble woman, with whom she lived on terms of unusual intimacy and affection, Anne Geneviève at a very early age fell under the spell of the Carmelite nuns, who were to remain her friends through life.

The history of the great Paris convent of that remarkable order, which sheltered the touching repentance of Mademoiselle de La Vallière and of so many others, is a striking one. When St. Teresa, their great reformer, died in 1582, her Spanish spiritual daughters had attained the height of their great reputation for saintliness. A remarkable Frenchwoman, Madame Acarie, induced a few of them to come to Paris for the purpose of founding a convent there and establishing their order in France. The result was, in the first instance, the 'Great Convent' in the Faubourg St. Jacques, the old quarter on the left bank of the Seine, far beyond the Luxembourg and all the places visited by foreigners. Very little is now left of the extensive buildings and fine old gardens of which it consisted. But the old spirit survives in the small community which took it up after the Revolution, and the order has since spread in all directions, so that it has now both a new house in the capital and convents throughout the length and breadth of the land.

At the time of which we are speaking their religious house is described as 'a little heaven upon earth' of the highest Christian virtues and the noblest traditions of the foundress, carried on by the great and good French nuns who continued the work after the departure of the Spanish mothers. Victor Cousin [1] has transcribed the biographies, compiled for purposes of edification and preserved in the old convent, of many of the distinguished women who, after shining in the world, had taken refuge in that austere haven of rest. It is a very interesting collection, and shows the power and fervour of the religious life in France in the seventeenth century, as well as the high level of culture and mental elevation of the women of that period.

The rule which excluded from the cloister those living in the world was strictly enforced, with a few exceptions in favour of 'foundresses' and benefactresses. Thus the Queen-Regent, Anne of Austria, who was styled first foundress, was a frequent visitor with Louis XIV. as a

[1] Victor Cousin, *La Jeunesse de Madame de Longueville.*

child, and the Princesse de Condé enjoyed the same privilege as one of the earliest and most generous benefactresses. She both visited the nuns and made frequent retreats in their house. So it came about that her daughter spent much of her time in the Great Convent. She became and always remained devoted to it, and as a mere child resolved herself to become a Carmelite. In addition to the reverence and admiration with which the exalted character of the nuns and the ascetic beauty of their lives filled Mademoiselle de Bourbon, other powerful early impressions confirmed her in the longing to fly from a world she hardly knew.

When she was thirteen, in 1632, her mother's brother, Henri Duc de Montmorency, was publicly beheaded [1] at Toulouse, by order of Richelieu, amidst manifestations of indignant devotion on the part of the people and his own followers. He had joined Gaston, Duke of Orleans and brother of Louis XIII., in the conspiracy of the malcontents, a fateful pre-

---

[1] Arrêt de Mort de Henri duc de Montmorency, Toulouse, 30 octobre, 1632, 4850, fol. 379 (*Bibliothèque Nationale*).

cursor of the civil wars of the *Fronde*, which were destined to be so disastrous to her and hers. Gaston betrayed him, as he invariably betrayed his friends when there was any danger to himself, and Montmorency became a victim to the merciless but absolutely statesmanlike policy of the great Cardinal. Anne Geneviève never forgot this tragedy in her own family.

Naturally enough nothing would induce the Prince de Condé to consent to his only daughter taking the irrevocable step, and when it became clear that, in spite of her extreme youth, her vocation was very strong, he and the Princess resolved to compel her to go into society. Her mind was set on other things; but to her mother, who reproached her with the scant trouble she took to make herself agreeable, she made the pretty and characteristic little speech so often quoted: 'You have, madame, a grace and charm so irresistible that, as I go nowhere without you and appear only after you, people cannot see any in me.' In spite of this line of argument it was arranged that heroic measures should be tried.

On February 16, 1635, King Louis XIII.
gave a ball at the Louvre, to which all the great
beauties of the nobility had been invited.
Three days before Anne Geneviève was
informed that she would be expected to go
to this, her first ball. Deeply alarmed, she
hastened to her friends, the Carmelites, and
implored them to advise what she should do.
The good mothers held a council on this
important question, and it was solemnly decided
that Mademoiselle de Bourbon must submit to
the parental will, but that, before adorning
herself as much as might be required of her,
she should put on, in self-defence against
the dangers and seductions of the world, 'a
little hair shirt.' And this was done accordingly.

She was already, at fifteen, extremely beautiful. In the words of Madame de Motteville,
'Mademoiselle de Bourbon, although very
young, was beginning to show the first signs of
the charms of that angelic face which has since
been the admiration of all,' and the family portrait
by du Cayer, painted in 1654, which has been

preserved at Versailles, and in which she stands between her father and mother, fully bears out these enthusiastic expressions. Her appearance at this memorable ball was one long triumph, and the little aspirant to the ascetic life returned from it an altered being. The world and its pleasures had laid hold of her, and her parents' fears were at an end. But the strong impressions of childhood, the love of everything that was best and most unselfish, and the deep religious fervour of these early days, remained latent in the brilliant girl, in the great leader of society, and the ambitious politician of her later years, until they were fanned into flame again in early middle life, and burnt brightly to the end.

By the side of a healthy love of the ordinary pleasures of society the taste for all things intellectual and literary became more and more developed in Anne Geneviève. The great, though by no means the only, centre of intellectual life was the Hôtel de Rambouillet. When Catherine de Vivonne, Marquise de Rambouillet, soon after her marriage, founded

the first *salon* known to history, the wars of the
Ligue, which had filled the reign of Henri IV.
with their rough earnestness, were over, and
that reaction towards general refinement and
love of the things of the mind was setting in
which was characteristic of the reign of his son,
Louis XIII., and of the real sovereign, Richelieu.
The Hôtel de Rambouillet was the first centre,
as it were, in which this new tendency found
expression. The fact that the literary discus-
sions there, when they happened to be guided
by Voiture and Ménage, occasionally descended
to triviality, matters but little, for the notion of
culture grew up there. The atmosphere was
saturated with it, and from the *ruelle* of
Madame de Rambouillet and her daughter,
Julie d'Angennes, it radiated in all directions
during the most brilliant years of its existence,
from 1620 to 1648.

The Hôtel de Rambouillet has been
described so often that one feels some hesita-
tion in going over the same ground. But,
nevertheless, its history is not very well known,
and many are still inclined to confound the

charming and remarkable type of the genuine *Précieuses* with the brilliant caricatures of their crude imitators in Molière's 'Précieuses Ridicules.'

The foundress of the Hôtel de Rambouillet was a woman of the greatest merit, good, clever, and devoted to things intellectual, gifted with a tact as perfect as her literary taste, who never hurt any one, was never touched by slander, and was beloved, without exception, by everybody who came across her. There is no portrait of her in existence, but we know from recorded contemporary opinion, and from the descriptions, in Mademoiselle de Scudéry's 'Le Grand Cyrus,' of Madame de Rambouillet under the name of 'Cléomire,' that she was beautiful and gifted with an unusually fine presence. Born in 1587, she was married in 1600 to Charles d'Angennes, Marquis de Rambouillet, with whom she lived on terms of the greatest affection. Both her sons died, one of them in the battle of Nortlingen, and three of the daughters became nuns. The other two, Julie and Angélique, in their different ways, helped to make their mother's *salon* the great historical institution it became.

Madame de Rambouillet had herself designed and built the beautiful house in the Rue St. Thomas du Louvre on entirely new and original lines of her own. It was the first ever constructed with a view to 'receiving' in it, the rooms being so disposed that one led out of the other; and the celebrated *Chambre Bleue*, so called because its walls were covered with blue velvet, which was the first room ever decorated in that colour, had had everything in it carefully thought out with reference to its destination as the principal reception-room. In it was arranged, a little later on, the *alcôve* which has caused amusement to succeeding generations. Its object was, however, an entirely practical one. The Marquise, when still quite young, became subject to an ailment which made it impossible for her to expose herself to the rays of the sun or to the heat of the fire. Hence she had to seek shelter in a comparatively dark and draughtless recess. Before this necessity arose, at twenty years old, she had resolved no longer to go to Court, or anywhere else, but always to be 'at home' to her friends.   By about 1617 or the following year her *salon* had taken shape, and for nearly thirty years it remained the most remarkable one ever known.   Madame de Rambouillet made her house the common ground of all those who possessed any distinction, in whatever rank, provided it was coupled with good manners.   Hence the familiar terms on which met under her roof the princes of the Blood-Royal, Madame de Sévigné and the aristocratic world in which she moved, and Ménage, Voiture, Chapelain, Sarrasin, Corneille, Mademoiselle de Scudéry and her brother—in fact men and women of mark belonging to almost every grade of the social scale.   The slight *préciosité* of the hostess, to which her younger daughter also inclined before it was exaggerated by others, helped to produce that exquisite polish of language and manners which the reign of Louis XIV. reduced to rules and generalised.   Withal she possessed that simplicity without which there can be no perfect

breeding ; and—a point which should be borne
in mind—thanks to the charming naturalness
and sense of humour of the Marquise and of
her daughter Julie, the Hôtel de Rambouillet
was never in any sense *le monde où l'on
s'ennuie*, but a place which all the best society,
young and old, clever and even insignificant,
thought the most delightful resort in the world—
far more so, if only one might have the *entrée*,
than any of the gorgeous entertainments the
Court or the town could provide.

It is not difficult to imagine that Mademoiselle de Bourbon found herself in her element
in such surroundings.   By the natural brilliancy
of her untutored mind, and the solid literary
judgment she possessed at an early age, she
had conquered a unique position for herself,
and she eventually became one of the arbiters
of taste of the Hôtel de Rambouillet.   Mademoiselle de Scudéry's faithful attachment to
her and hers originated there.   The ten
volumes of her 'Grand Cyrus' are now un-
readable.   Nevertheless, not only does that
extraordinary book, which was the precursor of

Madame de La Fayette's immortal 'Princesse de Clèves,' contain, as such, the germ of the modern psychological novel, but, since the discovery by Cousin of a 'key,' [1] it has become an historical document of considerable importance. We know now that the hero, 'Le Grand Cyrus' himself, was meant for Condé, and the heroine, 'Mandane,' for Madame de Longueville, whom the two Scudérys so disinterestedly admired and so chivalrously defended through good and evil report.

It was also at the Hôtel de Rambouillet Anne Geneviève formed a lifelong friendship with the celebrated Marquise de Sablé, whose name is inseparable from the 'Maxims' of La Rochefoucauld ; and thither her eldest brother and dearest friend, the Duc d'Enghien, constantly accompanied their mother and herself when, at the end of his severe course of studies, he was allowed to appear in society under the wing of the Princess.

Physically, as well as in the quality of their minds, the brother and sister, who resembled

[1] Victor Cousin, *La Société Française au XVIIème Siècle.*

each other in the grandeur of their characters, were very different. There was, even when he was quite young, a soldierly roughness in the speech and appearance of the Duc d'Enghien. He was not handsome, although he had that indefinable peculiarity, *le grand air*, as well as a fine head, a varying expression in the fiery blue eyes, whose colour was like that of his sister's, an abundance of wavy hair, and a well-proportioned, well-shaped figure. He was apt to be plain-spoken, though his manners were perfect, and his literary tastes inclined strongly to Corneille, whose magnificent language and strength of sentiments he thoroughly appreciated.

The beauty of Mademoiselle de Bourbon, while heightened by the freshness of perfect health, was nevertheless of an exquisite and somewhat ethereal type. All her portraits, of which the best is in the Salle des Bourbons at Versailles, show her with silky golden curls, a transparently white and pink complexion, brilliant blue eyes, a royally fine figure and carriage, and the most beautiful arms and

shoulders.   Whoever saw her dwelt on these
particular features, and the expression ' angelic,
as applied to her face, recurs again and again
in the memoirs of her contemporaries, whether
they be great ladies, men of letters, or divines.
Throughout her life one of the characteristics
of her intense charm was that it appealed to
men and women alike.   There was the same
delicate refinement in her mind and unfailing
taste ; and this was so fully recognised that,
later on, in the famous quarrel as to the
respective merits of the two sonnets, by
Benserade and by Voiture, which divided the
Court and the Academy, it was the fact that
Madame de Longueville had taken the part
of the latter which determined his ultimate
triumph.

Madame la Princesse herself had a most
brilliant circle, and what we should now call a
salon at the Hôtel de Condé, which also stood
in the Rue St. Thomas du Louvre, pulled down
many years ago to make room for the Place du
Carrousel.   There were constantly splendid re-
ceptions at the Louvre, at the Palais Cardinal, and

at all the great houses of the *noblesse* in Paris. In the summer Mademoiselle de Bourbon accompanied her mother to Court at Fontainebleau. They visited Rueil, the residence of Richelieu, besides other great country seats. But, above all, they spent much of their time at Chantilly, which is more intimately connected with the family of Condé than with that of Montmorency, to whom it belonged, until Charlotte Marguerite brought it into the more illustrious of the two great houses.

Its history is something of an epic, and its last owner and restorer, himself a hero, was also the distinguished historian of the powerful race to whom he was so nearly related. In those days the Château de Chantilly, built a little before the Renaissance, was not the palatial residence, containing wonderful collections, which, thanks to the Duc d'Aumale, it is now. When ' le Grand Condé' retired to the favourite seat of his family, where he ended his life, he turned the woods by which it was surrounded into the present lovely park. All this was yet to come. At the time we are speaking of the place was simply an ideal country house. Madame la Princesse, who spent the greater part of the summer there with her children, used to bring with her a troop of young people, the particular friends of the latter. To these were added Voiture, when he could be got, Sarrasin, and other *beaux esprits* of the time. The days were spent in delightful excursions, the reading aloud of novels and poetry, and in conversation, music, and the prettiest and most courteous flirtations, if indeed that term may be applied to the *galanterie* of those stately days. All the future heroes of Condé's great battles were there to be found. Among the girl-friends of Mademoiselle de Bourbon were Julie d'Angennes and the two sisters du Vigean. Marthe, the younger, was the one great and pure passion of Condé's youth. Her beauty, which was less striking than that of some of the more brilliant girls who surrounded her, seems to have been of a peculiarly appealing type. She was very gentle and retiring, very exclusive in her affections. Entirely devoted to the Duc d'Enghien, she was as entirely virtuous and dignified in her conduct. Although of a good old family, she was not considered of sufficiently high rank for a prince of the blood, and, with that businesslike and inflexible decision which characterised Monsieur le Prince—a genuine tyrant, albeit a well-meaning one—he refused to listen to his son's entreaties that he should be allowed to marry Mademoiselle du Vigean. In 1641, in spite of his most energetic resistance to the project, he was compelled to be married to Clémence de Maillé-Brézé, a niece of Cardinal de Richelieu. He would not live with her for a long time, and fell seriously ill from grief and disappointment. He roused himself only when his country had need of him.

The devotion of the victor of Rocroy for Marthe du Vigean remained for a long time as exalted as ever. He could hardly bear to be away from her, and made vain endeavours to get his marriage annulled. The ambition and love of emoluments of his father stood in his way, even when Cardinal Mazarin, who was in power by that time, might have been disposed to help him. As for her, she refused every other marriage that was proposed to her.

At last, after the difficult victory of Nort-lingen, followed by another illness, the Duc d'Enghien, despairing of ever bringing the early romance of his life to a happy termination, 'resolved to dismiss the matter from his mind,' and succeeded. But Madame de Motteville, who was well informed, assures us it was the only real love of his life. Marthe du Vigean never complained, but, in the fulness of her beauty and with an unstained reputation, at twenty-five buried her life in the Great Convent of the Carmelites.

Madame de Longueville remained in touch and on affectionate terms with her ever after, and never ceased to interest herself, for her sake, in the fortunes of her sister and to help to advance them.

The great question of the marriage of Mademoiselle de Bourbon had for some time been uppermost in the minds of her parents. She was quite young when she was first

betrothed to François de Lorraine, Prince de
Joinville, the eldest son of the Duc de Guise. In
fact that union had been contemplated, apparently, since she was less than a year old.[1] Such an
alliance would have been all that could be desired.
But the young Prince had to follow his father,
who faithfully accompanied Marie de Médicis to
Italy in her disgrace, and there he died in 1639.
Other marriages were now discussed, but it
was impossible to find a husband whose rank
entirely satisfied the Prince de Condé. At last
his choice and that of the Princesse fell on the
greatest personage in France next to the
princes of the blood. This, unfortunately,
happened to be the Duc de Longueville.

Henri II., Duc de Longueville, who was
born in 1595, was descended from the Comte
de Dunois,[2] the famous ' Bastard of Orleans,'
who fought by the side of Joan of Arc.

His father was Henri I. d'Orléans, second

---

[1] Contrat de Mariage de François de Lorraine, Prince de
Joinville, et d'Anne Geneviève de Bourbon, 25 février, 1620.—
4330, fol. 117 (*Bibliothèque Nationale*).

[2] Généalogie de la Maison d'Orléans-Longueville.—4067,
fol. 63 (*Bibliothèque Nationale*).

Duke,[1] and Prince of Neuchâtel and Vallengin. His mother, Catherine de Gonzague, sister of the Duc de Nevers, was the aunt of Marie de Gonzague, Queen of Poland, and Anne, the celebrated Princess Palatine.

The future husband of Anne Geneviève had been previously married to Louise de Bourbon, daughter of the Comte de Soissons, who died in 1637, and by whom he had had a daughter, Mademoiselle de Longueville. She eventually married the Duc de Nemours, who succeeded to the title after it had been borne by his two brothers. She was almost the same age as her stepmother, and speedily became her enemy, as is amply proved by the undisguised malice of her memoirs concerning the *Fronde*.

The Duc de Longueville was a *grand seigneur*, generous and brave, but of a vacillating disposition and easily led. He was forty-seven when he was married to Mademoiselle de

---

[1] Erection du Comté de Dunois en duché et pairie de France par Madame Louise Régente, en faveur de Louis d'Orléans ... Lyon, 1525. Ancien Fonds, 4587, fol. 64 (*Bibliothèque Nationale*).

Bourbon, who was twenty-two ; and he had,
moreover, still at the time an entanglement
with the notorious Duchesse de Montbazon.

There was much heartburning caused by the
event, for many of the men of her world were
in love with Anne Geneviève, among others the
Duc de Beaufort ; and he at any rate had
believed himself entitled to aspire to her hand.
She herself viewed the marriage with the
greatest reluctance.   But, of course, her feelings
were the last thing to be considered in so
important a matter.   The only point which
deserved the most careful attention was that
Mademoiselle de Bourbon should not derogate
or lose any of the privileges of her position.
Accordingly, by a special *Brevet* obtained by her
parents, she was allowed to retain all the prerogatives of a princess of the Blood-Royal
irrespective of the claims, always subject to
dispute, on account of the original *bar-sinister*,
which the Duc de Longueville possessed, the
first Duke having in 1571 received for his
descendants the title of princes of the blood.

This decree of Charles IX. was confirmed by letters patent in 1653.

On June 6, 1642, the marriage took place. 'La Grande Mademoiselle' (Anne-Marie-Louise d'Orléans, Duchesse de Montpensier in her mother's right, and daughter of Gaston, Duc d'Orléans) thus expresses the view society took of the event:

' It was a cruel destiny for her (Mademoiselle de Bourbon). M. de Longueville was old ; she was young, and beautiful as an angel.'[1]

She behaved like a princess and a great lady, and on her wedding-day her appearance was more dazzling than ever and her cheerfulness and exquisite courtesy to all as perfect as it had always been.

Shortly afterwards Madame de Longueville was attacked by the prevailing disease, smallpox, through which she was faithfully and fearlessly nursed by Mademoiselle de Rambouillet, and great was the excitement in society as to whether she would be marked or not. Cardinal

[1] *Mémoires de Mademoiselle.*

D

de Retz informs[1] us of the fact, much welcomed in her own particular world, that the complaint, 'while it took away the first flower of her beauty, did not injure its brilliancy.'

During the winter of 1643 the young Duchess led much the same pleasant and interesting life which had been hers as a girl, interrupted occasionally, for a short time, when she accompanied her husband to Normandy, of which province he was governor. The Hôtel de Rambouillet was at the height of its reputation. The poems which were collected to form the 'Guirlande de Julie' date from about that time. The Court and the great houses vied with each other as to which should display the greatest magnificence during this period of peace at home and glory abroad, destined so soon to come to an end. Madame de Longueville was surrounded by the homage and admiration of all. She was now considered an authority on all things literary. She herself possessed unusual conversational powers, and that which in contemporary parlance was

---

[1] *Mémoires du Cardinal de Retz.*

described as *le tour*—that is, an individual and characteristic way of expressing herself. Withal she was an admirable listener. Her courtesy and the manner of directing a general conversation, which were natural to her, amounted to an unconscious fine art, and the often-mentioned 'languor' in her speech and her whole personality seem to have added to her charm in the eyes of all who knew her.

Madame de Longueville was, and long remained, a coquette, in the unobjectionable sense of the term, for she was never a heartless one. Her wish to please, though tempered by pride and great personal dignity, was as marked a feature as that love of influence and desire to be first which, afterwards, developed in a manner so fatal to herself and others.

Her heart had never been touched, but she would seem to have shown a liking for one of her brother's friends, Maurice de Coligny, son of the Field-marshal de Châtillon, who had been one of those most anxious to marry her. He was, so far as one can tell, not very remarkable, but pleasing. He possessed the confidence of the Duc

d'Enghien, was an intimate friend of La Rochefoucauld, then Prince de Marsillac, and
remained faithfully devoted to Madame de
Longueville to his dying day. This young
man became mixed up in the most tragic way
with an episode in her life which, trivial in
itself, can only be appreciated in the light of
the real importance conferred on it by circumstances, if the political situation at the time is
duly taken into account.

Richelieu died on December 4, 1642, after
having witnessed, taking it as a whole, the
triumph of his policy. But when he had dis-
appeared the party of dissatisfaction raised its
head again. Louis XIII., who faithfully continued his great Minister's methods, died a year
after him. His successor was a child of four
years old. The Regency was left in the hands
of a Spanish princess, Anne of Austria, assisted
by a badly constituted Council, whilst the
northern frontier of France was threatened by
the Spaniards. Factions were ready to begin
civil war at the first opportunity, for the malcontents of the preceding reign had returned

from exile or imprisonment after Richelieu's death and formed the party of the ' Importants.' The safety of the country was in the hands of two men : the successor the great Cardinal had trained and chosen for himself, Mazarin, and the youthful Commander-in-Chief Louis XIII had given to his army, namely, the Duc d'Enghien, who, on the day when the King's body was carried to St. Denis, by a marvel of strategy won the battle of Rocroy.

The pride and glory of the House of Condé were therefore at their height, and an insult to its best-beloved member was an offence that could only be wiped out in blood.

Since his marriage the Duc de Longue-ville had been compelled by the Princesse de Condé to give up, to a certain extent, his relations to the Duchesse de Montbazon. This fact, and the way in which her undoubted, but far from refined, beauty was outshone by that of Madame de Longueville, had secured for the latter the revengeful hatred of her husband's former mistress. She had got under her sway the Duc de Beaufort, whose

passion for Madame de Longueville had been
coldly met, and the Duc de Guise, who had
become one of the leaders of the ' Importants.'
One evening, at a reception in Madame de
Montbazon's house, a certain Marquis de
Maulevrier dropped from his pocket two
compromising but unsigned letters from a
Madame de Fouquerolles. The lady of the
house, seeing her opportunity, declared they
had been dropped by Maurice de Coligny, and
that they were in the handwriting of Madame
de Longueville. The unfortunate Marquis de
Maulevrier having taken Marsillac into his
confidence, the latter succeeded in getting the
documents out of Madame de Montbazon's
hands, and, after showing them to the Prince
and Princesse de Condé, Madame de Sablé and
others, so as to establish the innocence of
Madame de Longueville, burnt them in the
presence of the Queen. Unfortunately the
matter was not allowed to drop. In spite of
the wishes of her daughter, who was always
very far removed from any petty pique, and of
the Duc de Longueville, whose position in the

affair was no enviable one, Madame la
Princesse insisted on a public reparation.   The
Queen was obliged to consent, and in her
presence Mazarin drew up, after endless
deliberations, the speech by which the offend-
ing Duchess was to be compelled to apologise
in person to the mother of her victim.   The
scene came off accordingly, and in the presence
of the Cardinal, on behalf of Anne of Austria,
Madame de Montbazon read her speech,
which had been fastened to her fan, with the
worst possible grace.   But the storm was by no
means allayed.   After sundry pin-pricks, it all
ended in a refusal on the part of the Duchess,
on an occasion when the Queen was accompanied by the Princesse de Condé, to comply
with the Regent's request that she should
withdraw, whereupon she received an order
from the King to leave Paris immediately.
The affair now became a party question with
the 'Importants,' and the Duc de Beaufort
entered into a conspiracy against Mazarin.

The latter had calmly and successfully
pursued the difficult policy of winning the

confidence of the Queen-Regent, by which means alone he could hope to accomplish his purpose of carrying out Richelieu's ideas. He showed her the dangers of the situation in their true light, and on September 2, 1643, the blow was struck which put an end to the intrigues of the malcontents. The Duc de Beaufort himself was arrested and imprisoned at Vincennes. His father, the Duc de Vendôme, was sent to his place in the country, together with his eldest son; and the whole party became disorganised, so that for some years internal peace prevailed.

Meanwhile the Duc d'Enghien returned victorious from the Rhine. He fiercely resented the insult done to his sister, but the Duc de Beaufort could not be called to account because he was in prison. Coligny, however, whom he trusted, and who had so far kept out of the way, lest he should help to compromise Madame de Longueville, and also because he had been dangerously ill, now reappeared on the scene. He wished to call out the Duc de Guise, Madame de Mont-

bazon's other *cavaliere servente*, who had been
mixed up in the unpleasant business, and,
according to La Rochefoucauld, the Duc
d'Enghien 'left him free to do so.' The
encounter took place in December, as usual, in
the Place Royale, in defiance of Richelieu's
fierce edict against duelling, which had become
one of the greatest plagues of society, and
swallowed up each year untold numbers of
the most valuable lives. The hereditary feud
between the houses of Coligny and Lorraine,
the latter of which was represented by the
Duc de Guise, lent a kind of epic flavour
to this unfortunate incident. Maurice de
Coligny's physical weakness made him an easy
victim for the superior skill of his adversary,
and he did not survive his fatal wound long
enough for the law to take its course.

This first tragedy in the life of Madame de
Longueville was made the subject of songs and
romances, and a legend grew up about it.
Some went so far as to suggest that she
watched the desperate fight of which she was
the cause, and to impugn her relations to

Coligny. It is quite certain, however, that neither of these things was true, and that until the time when the one great passion of her life began she had been blameless in the eyes of all who knew her well. With this one exception, even slander had not dared to sully her reputation.

She was now twenty-five. Up to this time Madame de Longueville had had two children. Her eldest daughter, Charlotte Louise, styled Mademoiselle de Dunois, was born on February 4, 1644, and her eldest son, Jean Louis Charles d'Orléans, Comte de Dunois, on January 12, 1646. Another daughter, Marie Gabrielle, was born in 1647, and her second son, Charles Paris, came into the world much later, in the most extraordinary circumstances, during the *Fronde*. Both the girls died in infancy, as was the way with the children of the great. Apparently, the nearer they were to the throne, the smaller their chances of life. Only one of the six children of Louis XIV. and Marie-Thérèse survived, and to readers of St. Simon's memoirs the wonder is how they ever lived through the management and the etiquette to which they were subjected. In their early years children played no part in the lives of their parents in those days ; but for the time being the Duchesse de Longueville seems to have felt the loss of her daughters a good deal.

In spite of the shock involved in the death for her of Maurice de Coligny, her life was still as brilliant and enjoyable as ever. The principal change, or fresh development in her character, which was too strong to be satisfied only with personal homage, was the element of ambition, not as yet for herself, but for her brother. Such, at any rate, was the view taken by Mazarin.

In his 'Carnets,' written in Italian and Spanish, and intended only for the Queen's perusal, he describes Madame de Longueville in the severest and most hostile terms, entirely losing sight of the good and great points in her character. But, as an instance of his marvellous foresight, this 'portrait,' which probably dates from about 1644, just after the famous duel, is well worth quoting :

'The said lady is all-powerful with her bro-ther.   She prides herself on looking down upon the Court, on hating favours, and despising all those she does not see at her feet.   She would fain see her brother at the head of everything and having all favours at his own disposal.   She well knows how to conceal what she is doing. She receives every act of deference and every favour as if it were her due.   She is generally very cold to people, and if she likes *la galanteria*, it is not in the least because she means any harm, but merely in order that she may win friends and followers for her brother.   She suggests to him ambitious thoughts, to which he already sufficiently inclines.   She does not consider her mother much, because she believes her to be attached to the Court.   Like her brother, she looks upon every favour as a debt which is paid to herself, her house, her relations, and her friends.   She thinks they would be willingly refused to them, but that nobody dares to displease them.   She has close rela-tions with the Marquise de Sablé and the Duchesse de Lesdiguières.   At Madame de Sablé's house, d'Andilly, the Princesse de Guéménée, Enghien and his sister, Nemours, and many others, constantly meet, and the talk there is very free.   Some one should be found to give information as to what goes on there.'

This highly prejudiced view of Anne-Geneviève's disposition is also a very much more serious one than that conveyed by any other contemporary writer, and exceedingly interesting in the light of subsequent events.

In 1645 Monsieur de Longueville, whose official appointments already included, besides the governorship of Normandy, the position of member of the Council of Regency, was sent as Plenipotentiary to the Congress of Münster. He was a highly ornamental Ambassador, and on the whole acquitted himself well and with great dignity of his difficult diplomatic functions. But Mazarin was much annoyed at the prolonged delay in his going to take up his post, which he attributed, perhaps rightly, to the reluctance of the Duchess to leave Paris. Her husband had become deeply attached to her in time. No one could ever resist her personal fascination. He was, therefore, most anxious that she should accompany him ; and she was equally so not to exchange the scene of her brilliant life for the grey sky of Westphalia. Her health furnished a sufficient excuse during the winter, and finally the Duke had to start alone. In the following spring, however, Madame de Longueville yielded, and, amidst the lamentations of the Hôtel de Rambouillet and all her circle, she began her triumphal progress to Münster, accompanied by her stepdaughter, then a girl of twenty, on June 20, 1646.

It was a magnificent pageant from beginning to end. She had a numerous escort of the Duke's own guards. At every stage there were ovations and ceremonies. The governors of all the towns through which she passed came out to meet her at the head of their garrisons. The keys of many of them were offered to her. On the Rhine, Turenne, the greatest of Condé's pupils in the art of war and, after him, the greatest captain of the age, enacted before her the magnificent spectacle of an army ranged for battle and manœuvring for her amusement. He was passionately in love with her in 1650, and remained her slave for years, but the first impression was probably produced on this occasion. The Duke, who had made the most elaborate preparations to ensure her having a splendid reception, came to meet his wife at a considerable distance from Münster. Her entry into the city was that of a queen, and a queen the beautiful Duchess remained during the whole of her stay within its walls. The letters, not only of literary Frenchmen writing home, but of Spaniards, Italians, and other delegates and distinguished persons, convey the impression that she was the centre of everything, that no one had eyes for anybody else, and that every human being who approached her raved about her beauty, her charm and dignity, and her brilliant mind. At Monsieur de Longueville's suggestion she broke the monotony of her stay by a journey into Holland, which interested her and was the means of bringing about an interview between her and the Princess Elizabeth, Queen of Bohemia and sister of Charles I., through whom Queen Victoria is descended from the Stuarts.

Meanwhile all her Paris worshippers and friends were recalling Madame de Longueville in prose and verse. Whilst she was at Münster,

in the autumn of 1646 came the great news of
the surrender of Dunkirk to the Duc d' Enghien,
one of his greatest achievements, which gave a
considerable impulse to the weighty and pro-
tracted negotiations. At the end of December
of the same year she received the intelligence
of the fateful death of her father. This was a
great blow to the House of Condé, which lost
in him a head who was the incarnation of
practical good sense, and quite free from that
hot-tempered impulsiveness which led astray all
its other members. Had he lived longer he
would probably have saved them from the dis-
asters they brought upon themselves and upon
France.

This event and the fact that another child
was soon to be born supplied Madame de
Longueville with an excuse for returning to
Paris; and this she did, after a short rest at
Chantilly. Her arrival was acclaimed as an
event. Among her many worshippers from
that time forward must be counted her younger
brother, the Prince de Conti, who had then
just finished his studies, and in 1647, at eighteen

made his first appearance in society. He formed part of the little court of his sister, who, save during a short interval, ruled him completely, for good and evil, as long as he lived.

Paris was steeped in festivities. It was the time when Mazarin, to please the Queen, gave the most marvellous entertainments, balls and operas, imported from Italy. The Hôtel de Rambouillet was fast approaching the end of its career, but the last phase was still a bright one. Madame de Longueville had again become the cynosure of all eyes. This is how Madame de Motteville describes her at this, perhaps the most brilliant, period of her life:

'That Princess who, even when absent, reigned over her whole family, and whose approval was looked upon by all as the highest blessing, having returned to Paris, could not fail to appear there with even greater *éclat* than before she left. The affection Monsieur le Prince, her brother, entertained for her warranted her actions and her ways, and the greatness of her beauty and of her mind increased the influence of her family to such an extent that she had not been long at Court before she became the object of its undivided attention. . . . Her knowledge, her wit, and the

E

opinion entertained of her judgment caused her to be admired by every well-bred person, and all were convinced her good opinion alone could ensure their reputation.   In fact it may be safely said that at that time all greatness, glory, and *galanterie* were centred in that family of Bourbon whose head was Monsieur le Prince, and that happiness was no longer accounted a blessing unless it were bestowed by them.'

In the midst of all this brightness and prosperity there entered into the life of Anne-Geneviève de Bourbon the man for whom she conceived the one overwhelming passion of her life, and who was destined to be its evil genius.

François, Prince de Marsillac, the future Duc de la Rochefoucauld, and author of the ' Maxims,' was born on December 15, 1613. He was married to Mademoiselle de Vivonne, served in Italy and Flanders, and was wounded at the siege of Mardyk in 1646.   His father was the first Duke who owed his title to Marie de Medici, and remained faithful to her after her breach with Richelieu, so that his son grew up in an atmosphere of court intrigue and semi-conspiracy.   When, in his turn, the latter came to Court, he became a partisan of Queen Anne of Austria, in the days of her struggles with the Cardinal. When she was accused of siding with Spain, in 1637, and in danger of being disgraced and imprisoned, La Rochefoucauld tells us in his not over-reliable memoirs that she proposed to him he should carry off to Brussels herself and Mademoiselle de Haute-fort, with whom both he and the King were in love. Nothing came of this astonishing plan. He only got into trouble with Richelieu, and that very slightly, by helping Madame de Chevreuse, the Queen's favourite, who was in exile at Tours, to escape to Spain, and was afterwards indirectly connected with the conspiracy of Cinq-Mars. Nevertheless, when Queen Anne was in power as Regent he believed himself entitled to special rewards and consideration on the part of herself and Mazarin. This it is necessary to bear in mind for the better understanding of his subsequent conduct.

It is extremely difficult to form a just estimate of the complex character of the Duc de la Rochefoucauld, then only Prince de

Marsillac. To judge him by the earlier phases of his life—those which concern Madame de Longueville—he was a vain, mean, cowardly, self-seeking person, absolutely sceptical, like the view of human nature his 'Maxims' convey, capable of betraying and publicly slandering the woman who had sacrificed herself to him and his petty ambition. In his old age, his devoted and exemplary friendship for the object of his real love, Madame de La Fayette, when she was herself becoming old and infirm, went far to redeem his contemptible early life, and to show that something there must have been in his soul which justified an affection so strong and enduring that it is impossible to account for it by intellectual fascination alone. It was, nevertheless, the charm of his mind and wit which attracted Madame de Longueville, at any rate in the first instance. There is an enamel by Petitot, an engraving from which was reproduced as a frontispiece to one of the editions of the 'Maxims' (1778), which shows him to have been handsome. He was especially distinguished by his *grand air*, his courtesy, and the charm of his conversation, which rendered him irresistible to one who looked upon this as her favourite among the fine arts.

It was on her return from Münster that their close friendship began, and that he voluntarily and deliberately set about casting over her, for his own purposes, the spell she was unable to throw off. The perfect cynicism with which he himself avows and describes his conduct in his memoirs is not to be surpassed. It should be mentioned that he was never really compromised in any of the undertakings of the 'Importants,' being too vacillating, and at all times more of a critic than a man of action. But one cannot do better than quote his own account of his early relations to Madame de Longueville.

After describing his disgust at the semi-disgrace meted out to him by the Cardinal, and the vague promises and empty flatteries that were all he had obtained from the Queen, he goes on to say :

'So much that was useless, and so many

disappointments, drove me at last to entertain different thoughts, and induced me to be on the look-out for perilous ways and means of showing my resentment towards the Queen and Cardinal Mazarin. The beauty of Madame de Longueville, her wit, and all the charms of her person, attached to her all those who could have any hope of being tolerated by her. Many men and many women of quality endeavoured to please her; and, over and above the attractions of this kind of court, Madame de Longueville was at that time so perfectly at one with her house, and so tenderly beloved by her brother, the Duc d'Enghien, that the esteem and friendship of that Prince were assured to him who had the approval of his sister. Many people vainly attempted this road to success, and mixed up with it other feelings than those of ambition. Miossens, who afterwards became Marshal of France, persisted longest, and met with as little success as the rest. Being a particular friend of his, he kept me informed of his designs. They destroyed themselves very soon. He realised it was so, and told me he was resolved to give them up. But vanity, which was his strongest passion, frequently prevented his telling me the exact truth, and he feigned hopes he did not feel, and which I knew he could not have. Thus some time passed, and at last I had reason to think *that I might make better use of the friendship and confidence of Madame de*

Longueville. I made him acknowledge it himself. He knew how I was situated at Court. I explained my views, but that consideration for him would always stop me, and that I would never attempt to enter into intimate relations with Madame de Longueville unless he left me free to do so. I confess I purposely embittered him against her in order to secure her for myself, without, however, saying anything untrue. He handed her over to me altogether ; but he repented of having yielded her to me when he saw the sequel of this *liaison.*'

Brutal meanness can no further go, and, with the exception of Jean Jacques Rousseau's, in a different way, there is no more cynical confession on record.

From this time began the apparently chivalrous devotion of the Prince de Marsillac to the proud, high-spirited woman who had never fallen from her high estate before, but who, when she gave her heart to this man, gave herself altogether, and sacrificed to him her reputation, her family, her great love for her brother and her country.

Nothing could exceed the glory which the wise diplomacy of Mazarin and the splendid

victories of Condé had shed and were shedding
on France during those years. Each of the
achievements of *le Grand Condé*, with their
sequels of fine disinterestedness and care
for his armies and all those he thought
entitled to reward, brought the tedious negotiations at Münster a step further. At last the
victory of Lens, the crowning event of his
five campaigns on the Rhine, had for its
immediate result the great Treaty of Westphalia, concluded in 1648, and signed at
Münster on September 8, and at Osnabrück on
August 6, which brought the Thirty Years'
War to a close. The part of the treaty
signed at Münster was between France and
the Emperor, and the other between France
and Sweden. The victors mutually guaran-
teed each other's acquisitions and concessions
for their allies in the Empire.

To France was confirmed the possession
of Upper and Lower Alsace, together with
Haguenau, Sandgau, and Busnach; the
sovereignty of the three bishoprics of Metz,
Toul, and Verdun, which had long been hers

by right of conquest ; the right to garrison
Philipsbourg, and the sovereignty of Pignerol.
To Germany it gave peace and the cessation
of religious strife.   It left France with no other
enemy to face than Spain.

As this treaty gave France her natural
frontier in the east, so it was Mazarin's design
that another, with Spain, should secure for her
the same advantages in the south-west.   This
result was undoubtedly retarded—the Treaty
of the Pyrenees was not concluded till 1660—
and never accomplished as fully as he had been
justified in hoping that it would be, thanks to
the disastrous civil wars in which, under the
name of *la Fronde*, culminated the earlier
intrigues and conspiracies of the Regency.

For this great evil the House of Condé,
and in particular Madame de Longueville,
under the baneful influence of La Rochefoucauld,
are very largely responsible.

CHAPTER II

THE WARS OF THE FRONDE (FIRST PART)

THE Comte de Ste. Aulaire, in his ' History of the Fronde,' has attempted to rehabilitate the two civil wars known under that name, and to show that they were the precursors of the French Revolution. But this is a position which seems absolutely untenable when the events are considered in the light of the facts and of the motives of those who were the instigators of the disastrous struggles involved in them. The circumstance that, in the first instance, the great nobles who throughout were the leaders of the movement were supported by the ' Sovereign Companies,' consisting of magistrates who were the representatives of the people, and the most important of which was the Parliament of Paris, is the only one

which gives colour to the theory that interesting book was written to substantiate.   The
answer to the argument is that the real Fronde
was at first mixed up with the legitimate
rising of the people, supported by Parliament,
against Mazarin and the internal maladminis-
tration of his Government.   The nobles who
hated him found it convenient to join them, but
in their essence the popular movement and the
revolt of the aristocracy had nothing to do
with each other.   It is not too much to say
that their union was purely accidental.

In effect the wars of the Fronde, with the
exception of their commencement, were a duel
between two men.   One was the unscrupulous
but marvellously astute and able statesman
chosen by Richelieu to govern France after
him, because he knew that the successor of his
choice could and would make the country what
he himself had designed that it should become.
In carrying out this work he stood practically
alone but for the steadfast and courageous
support of Queen Anne of Austria.   To all
parties alike—to the princes, to the nobles and

to the people, for different reasons—he remained
the Italian adventurer, the hated intruder and
tyrant who had ruined the country by his incapacity in financial matters, and substituted
subtle and underhand revenge for the open,
high-handed cruelty of Richelieu, before whose
truly French genius they had unconsciously
bowed, even while he was feared by all classes
without distinction.   There is nothing pathetic
about the figure of Mazarin, but one cannot
but look with a sense of tragedy on the scene
when this man, who, in spite of all, had done
such great things, lay on his deathbed, whilst
around his palace the people were waiting
eagerly for the news of his death.   The nieces
and the nephew, who owed him everything,
but whose lives he had managed to make a
burden, were gloating over the prospect of their
approaching deliverance.   The Queen alone
bent over him affectionately and yearningly.   The
handsome Cardinal was not a priest, and there
is a good deal of evidence which corroborates
the supposition that he had become her
husband.   From her, his one faithful friend, of

whom he was hopelessly weary, he turned his face away.

His rival, not in statecraft, but in the love of intrigue and power, in unscrupulousness, in diplomatic skill, put to a different use, and deftness in flattering and directing women, while appearing to be swayed by them, was Jean François Paul de Gondi, afterwards Cardinal de Retz. Born in 1613, he was made to take orders against his will, and endeavoured to escape from the inevitable consummation by leading a dissolute life. Having finally resigned himself to his fate, he became a distinguished preacher, and was made Coadjutor to the Archbishop of Paris in 1643. Though a Frenchman in every respect, by a curious instance of atavism the blood of the Florentine ancestors of the Gondis comes out so strongly in this plain and almost insignificant-looking, intensely clever ecclesiastic, who managed by entirely Italian arts to govern and have at his back the nobility of France, that one involuntarily thinks of the whole struggle as a single combat between two cunning Italians, the one supported by the Regent, the other throughout by the nobles and the princes, and for a short time by the people and the Parliament. The object of that duel was, in the case of each of the combatants, to get unto his own side Louis de Bourbon, now Prince de Condé, whom both hated for his pride, his impulsive brusqueness, and his unrivalled power, whilst they believed that the weight of his sword would turn the scales in favour of that party which finally secured him.

Mazarin's policy, in its aims, was identical with that of Richelieu, which, indeed, the Minister of Louis XIII. had inherited from Louis XI., who broke the power of his great feudal vassals, and from Henri IV. He had crushed the nobles who were in power as governors of provinces or otherwise, just as he had openly and mercilessly trampled upon the Queen herself, through the instrumentality of her husband, when he suspected her of being in league with Spain. His successor, on the contrary, who governed through Anne of Austria, endeavoured to attract the aristocracy to the Court by making it as brilliant as possible, and thus to turn their thoughts from any political ambition, at the same time removing them from the castles that were still their strongholds. Being as bad an administrator and as reckless a financier as he was great as a foreign Minister and head of the Government, he distributed bribes, honours, and emoluments, according to the characters of the recipients, with an extravagance which very nearly landed the country in utter ruin. This was the secret of the co-operation between his adversaries and the Parliaments of the great cities. Originally they had possessed no powers to interfere in the affairs of the State. But the Queen had, to all intents and purposes, invested them with such powers by applying to the Parliament of Paris for the abrogation of the Council of Regency instituted by Louis XIII. The position of the Government was, therefore, one of excessive difficulty. After fresh vexatious duties had been imposed on supplies entering Paris, the Parliament assembled under the venerable magistrate,

Mathieu Molé. Having refused to register the new decrees, it made an order called *l Arrêt d' Union*, by which it undertook to meet in the Grand Council Chamber in the Cour des Comptes and Cour des Aides, for the purpose of deliberating on State affairs and reforming the Constitution, whereby it assumed the position of a political body. Mazarin declared this to be an attempt against the rights of the Crown, and upon the Parliament refusing to submit the Queen ordered the arrest of the three Presidents, Blancmênil, Charton, and Broussel. Thereupon the people of Paris rose, made barricades, and so com-
· pelled the Queen to release the prisoners and acquiesce in the demands of Parliament. It was in the thick of the popular protest against the arbitrary imprisonment of the magistrates that the Coadjutor first appeared on the scene, as a peacemaker to begin with, inclined to help the Court if he had met with encouragement in that quarter. The imprudently hostile attitude of the Regent, when he endeavoured to warn and advise her, induced

him to cast his lot with the opposite party. Instead of following his counsels of moderation, Mazarin and the Queen now resolved to put into practice the system of severity which the former had sketched out in his ' Carnets.' The first step was to get rid of Châteauneuf, a former Keeper of the Seals, persecuted by Richelieu, as a creature of Madame de Chevreuse, and of Chavigny, a former confidant of the late Cardinal's, to whom Mazarin was beholden, and who was a friend of the House of Condé. The former was sent into exile to his country house, and the latter imprisoned at Vincennes. On the same day the Queen left Paris, and took the King and his brother to St. Germain, whither Monsieur le Prince, who had joined them at Rueil, accompanied the Court. Up to that time he had been carefully kept at a distance, whilst being constantly consulted by Mazarin, because the wise and moderate views expressed in his letters to the Cardinal with reference to the dispute with Parliament did not meet with the approval of either Anne of Austria or her

F

Minister. On all sides attempts were made
to influence him ; but the most vigorous endeavours were those of his old acquaintance,
the Coadjutor of Paris, whom he put off at
last with the words, ' My name is Louis de
Bourbon, and I will not shake the power of
the Crown.'

Condé had not, however, as yet fully understood the bearing of the struggle that was going
on. At that particular moment the Parliament
of Paris, which had begun by standing up for
its own privileges, was the vindicator of the
rights of the people. It defended those two
fundamental guarantees of liberty, the right not
to be taxed without the people's own consent,
and the recognition of the principle that no
subject should be exposed to arbitrary deten-
tion.

In the Orders of the year 1648 Mazarin
admitted having spent in advance three years'
revenue, and the arrest of the councillors was
in defiance of an old ordinance unearthed by
the magistrates, according to which no one
could be imprisoned without being interrogated

within twenty-four hours and brought before his judges with the least possible delay.

Monsieur le Prince met with considerable harshness the deputation which had come to Rueil for the purpose of petitioning that the King might be brought back to Paris, and only told them to submit themselves unreservedly to the King. The Court received him with enthusiasm in consequence; but he soon began to see the true nature of the situation, and the necessity for compromise and timely concessions where right was on the side of the opposition. Neither the Minister nor a Spanish Princess imbued with the belief in the absolute power of the Sovereign was, however, accessible to such liberal ideas. Mazarin now showed himself the consummate actor he was. The delegates from the Parliament had been invited to St. Germain. The Assembly, invoking the declaration of 1617 against the Maréchal d'Ancre, refused to treat with a Minister who was a foreigner. He at once and to all appearances completely effaced himself, pretended to be of different opinion from the Queen, and

left Condé to bear the brunt of the attack.
The latter received the delegates on this occasion with his habitual charm and courtesy, and,
as Mazarin had foreseen, lost his temper as
soon as the discussion commenced. The Duc
d'Orléans, as usual, hesitated between threats
and concessions. The Duc de Longueville
and the Prince de Conti (always rather jealous
of his elder brother, and whom Madame de
Longueville had sent to counterbalance the
latter's influence) had to give way before Condé,
and although it was he who helped the delegates
to carry the day, he vexed and irritated them
past endurance by his pride and sarcasm. All
his life he possessed to the highest degree the
' gentle art of making enemies.' The practical
outcome of the conference was the important
declaration of October 22, 1648, which contained in effect all that the Sovereign Company
had demanded in regard to the control of taxa-
tion in every form, and practically, although
expressed in somewhat vague terms, what
amounted to an act of Habeas Corpus.

After endless difficulties the Queen's signature was obtained and the Court returned to Paris.

So far there can be no doubt that the parliamentary party was in the right, and that the cause of the people, which they represented, had justly triumphed. The agitation which followed had for its only possible excuse the belief that Mazarin would contrive to elude the undertaking signed at St. Germain. The attempt of the Parliament to play the part of a permanent political body, and thus to undermine the royal authority, completely changed the character of the revolution.

The hatred of Mazarin was so violent that it deprived wise old magistrates, as well as the nobles and the populace, of all sound judgment. The influence of the hero of so many victories was gone, partly no doubt on account of his hot and uncompromising temper, but mainly because he supported the Court and the detested Minister. Perhaps Mathieu Molé alone was sincerely friendly to Monsieur le Prince and the House of Condé.[1]

[1] *Mémoires de Mathieu Molé.*

For the time being there was a fairly good understanding between him and the ever-changeful Gaston, Duke of Orleans. Mazarin took advantage of that state of things to lay before them and the Queen's other advisers the plan at which he had hinted two months before. The Parliament and the Hôtel de Ville had made common cause, he said, and her Majesty had resolved to crush their rebellion. The King would leave his capital, and Paris would be blockaded and reduced to obedience by famine.

Condé absolutely and most wisely opposed this plan, which he considered disastrous. In his opinion the King must on no account leave Paris, and his own plan for restoring order was an admirably thought-out scheme for insuring the protection of the Court within the walls and the military occupation of the city. He was overruled, and on January 6, 1649, without any notice, and with elaborate precautions which gave it the appearance of a kind of flight, the Queen and her two sons left Paris, whither they did not return till the following August. They were protected by Condé and accompanied by the whole Court, including Madame la Princesse Douairière.

Madame de Longueville now took the first step which really foreshadowed the part she was about to play. Alleging as an excuse the state of her health, she declined to accompany the Court. The Duke, at his wife's suggestion, had gone to his province of Normandy in order to endeavour to bring about a rising of the population. The Prince de Conti, entirely under his sister's sway, had joined the insurgents. The Prince de Marsillac remained near Madame de Longueville.

When the Queen discovered this state of things she became much alarmed, and began to suspect a plot, and that Condé was involved in it. But his genuine indignation at what had been done by other members of his family convinced her eventually that she had been mistaken in regard to him. As a matter of fact, there had been differences between the sister and elder brother for some time, and when Madame de Longueville first declared herself for the Parliamentarians, he had formally refused to allow himself to be enrolled in the ranks of her party, as the Prince de Conti had done, whereupon a violent scene had taken place between the two most high-spirited and hot-headed members of the House of Condé.

To some extent, no doubt, the sympathy of a generous nature for the real grievances of the people influenced Madame de Longueville during this first part of the Fronde, which was so different in character from the sequel. Furthermore, Marsillac, whose sole objects, as already stated, were personal vengeance against Anne of Austria and her Minister, and certain advantages to be gained for himself, had succeeded in stirring up her natural love of authority and power, as well as the appearance of power. Her declared enemy, the Duchesse de Nemours, says, with some show of truth : [1]

'The strongest reason which determined her course, which was also the motive which touched her most, was that in thus entering on

---

[1] *Mémoires de Marie d'Orléans, Duchesse de Nemours.*

a great field of action she would be considered to possess even greater powers of mind, the one quality which was the object of her predominant passion and of her most pressing and dearest wishes. In a word, whatever she thought most likely to establish her personal merit always prevailed with her over every other consideration.'

Last, not least, the explanation is to be found in an element in her character which no one has described more accurately than the man who dragged her into a movement in which, ultimately, she could do nothing but harm.

He says of Madame de Longueville : [1]

' She combined in herself all the advantages of wit and beauty to such a degree, and in so attractive a shape, that it would seem nature had taken a pleasure in forming a perfect work. But those fine qualities were made less brilliant by one stain, which was never found before in a Princess of such great merit. It is that, so far from being a law unto those who really worshipped her, she so transformed herself by entering into their way of feeling that she no longer recognised her own as soon as they had succeeded in pleasing her.'

[1] *Mémoires du Duc de la Rochefoucauld.*

Thus La Rochefoucauld's own words dispose of the theory, so long commonly accepted, that it was Madame de Longueville who carried him away with her into this unhappy civil war, as she undoubtedly did her husband and brothers. The day when she was to turn Condé from the path of duty had not come as yet, and for the present the Coadjutor resolved to make the most of the disagreement between the brother and sister.

Energetic measures were now being taken to carry out the 'blockade.' Mazarin continually issued fresh orders for the stopping of supplies of food, which so far had got into Paris pretty freely in spite of the ordinances. Condé carried out the military arrangements, in accordance with a policy of which he disapproved, faithfully and successfully. The population soon began to suffer severely, and they made preparations to defend themselves. The 'generals' in command of the amateur troops were numerous. Among them were the Duc de Bouillon, head of the House of Turenne, Maréchal de la Motte Houdancourt,

La Boulaye, and that idol of the populace, the Duc de Beaufort, grandson of Henri IV. (his father, the Duc de Vendôme, was the son of Gabrielle d'Estrée, and was 'recognised' by the King). He had escaped from the dungeon of Vincennes in May 1648, and having received permission to reside at Anet, the place of his brother, who became the second Duc de Vendôme, he made his way to Paris on January 13 of the following year. A regular engagement took place at Charenton, in which on the Royalists' side the Duc de Châtillon, Condé's friend, was killed. Both the suffering and the disorders increased. The populace had begun to suspect that Madame de Longueville's motive for remaining in Paris was that, secretly, she was playing into the hands of Monsieur le Prince. In order to put an end to any feeling of that kind Gondi went to her and proposed that the Duchess and Madame de Bouillon, with their children, should come and reside at the Hôtel de Ville. It was a stroke of genius. 'Imagine,' he says himself,[1] 'these two ladies

---

[1] *Mémoires du Cardinal de Retz.*

on the terrace of the Hôtel de Ville, all the more beautiful because they appeared carelessly dressed, though they were not. Each held in her arms one of their children, who were as beautiful as their mothers. The *Grève* was full of people up to the roofs. All the men shouted for joy and the women shed tears of emotion.'

The presence among them of Madame de Longueville reassured the Parisians. All the great nobles who were in opposition paid their court to her, the Duc de Bouillon, the Duc d'Elbœuf, the Marquis de Noirmoutiers, as well as the magistrates. Marsillac was in attendance, as a matter of course, and in her room all the details of the programme of their party were discussed, and settled only with her approval.

In these extraordinary surroundings Madame de Longueville's second son and youngest child was born in the night from the 28th to the 29th of January, 1649. The following day she requested President Le Féron, in the name of 'Messieurs' of the Parliament, to act as godfather, with the Duchesse de

Bouillon, to the little boy, who was baptised Charles Paris in honour of his birthplace and styled the Comte de St. Pol. The ceremony was carried out with the greatest solemnity, the baby being carried in a procession to the church accompanied by magistrates, archers, and officials of various kinds, in their robes; after which the Marquis de Noirmoutiers brought him back to his mother, who had him conveyed with his nurses to the Hôtel de Condé.

The provinces were also suffering severely by this time. At last came the greatest wrong and the greatest calamity of all, in the shape of an attempt at foreign intervention, sanctioned by Parliament. An emissary of the Archduke Leopold was actually received by them. The excitement of the Court was very great indeed, and in a letter to Gérard Condé says :

' Things have reached such a pass that my brother has sent Bréquigny to Brussels to negotiate with the Archduke.[1] . . . This event has touched me extraordinarily, by the greatness

[1] Instruction du Prince de Conti à M. de Bréquigny pour l'Archiduc, 23 février, 1649. MS. Français, vol. 3854, fol. 19 (*Bibliothèque Nationale*).

of the evil that has been done in daring to treat with the King of Spain during a time of open war.'

It seems like a prophetic condemnation of his own future acts! To this was now added another catastrophe, as far as the Court was concerned, in the shape of a piece of unexpected good fortune to the *Frondeurs*. The Duc de Bouillon received the welcome intelligence that his brother, Turenne, had decided to join the party of rebellion and had addressed to his troops a manifesto which the Council of Regency justly declared to be treasonable. This step, which can in no way be reconciled with his well-known patriotism and admiring friendship for Condé, is more than difficult to explain. He never distinctly or intelligibly answered the questions put to him on the subject by the Coadjutor. The only interpretation of so extraordinary an act which has anything to recommend it is that he was undoubtedly very much in love with Anne-Geneviève de Bourbon, and that Turenne's temperament was of such a kind that he could

not help yielding to the impulse of the
moment.

Steps to ward off this fatal blow were taken
with laudable rapidity.   D'Erlac was appointed
to succeed him in his command, and the Prince
de Condé pledged his jewellery and precious
stones to a banker who was ready to make the
necessary advances.   By this means the army
continued to be paid, in spite of the empty
coffers of the treasury, and remained faithful to
the King.

The Archduke was on his way to invade
the country, in connivance with the very Parliament which had gloried in representing the
royal and national tradition.   Its glory had
passed away.   The good work it had done was
about to be undone, and it felt its own degrada-
tion.   As the sufferings increased which the
people of Paris, as well as the rural population,
had to endure under the system by which it
was proposed to reduce them to obedience,
they became less and less pliable instruments
in the hands of their Frondeur leaders.   The
only thing that remained was the fierce hatred

of 'le Mazarin.' The refusal to negotiate with him was maintained. But, nevertheless, on March 12 the Peace of Rueil was concluded between the two parties in the State. It was not registered, though until April 11 and during the period which intervened can be seen, for the first time, in all their meanness the small personal hagglings between Mazarin and the leaders of the Fronde, to whom honours and emoluments were recklessly conceded, with a more or less well-defined intention not to keep half the promises made.

Marsillac and Beaufort were of course foremost in the negotiations, which were discussed and planned in the room of Madame de Longueville, where, one regrets to think, the possibility of signing a treaty with Spain had been so recently contemplated. All the while Madame de Chevreuse, the former favourite of Anne of Austria, but now her enemy, was in Brussels, stirring up the Spanish authorities by representing to them that they were about to gain all their points. Spain was attacking France on all sides, and Condé alone faced every difficulty.

Under his safe escort the Court now removed from St. Germain to Compiègne. The army was calling for him, and the all-important question was, Would the general command be intrusted to him or not? Mazarin's petty hatred and distrust of him carried the day. He did not refuse to give the command to Condé, but by the line of conduct he prescribed he made it impossible for the latter to accept it. Monsieur le Prince generously proposed that it should be given to Turenne, but the Minister would not let bygones be bygones. Instead he appointed the insignificant Comte d'Harcourt, who was engaged in putting down the small rebellion the Duc de Longueville had succeeded in stirring up in Normandy. With patriotic disinterestedness Condé helped to instruct him and to carry out the measures of which he himself disapproved. In between whiles there had been at Chaillot an interview between Condé and the other members of his family, in which he became reconciled to his sister and the Prince de Conti, and there is good reason for supposing that already on that occasion she began to

G

recover some of her former influence over him. The Duc d'Orléans came back to Paris, and was well received; Monsieur le Prince, who did the same, was less fortunate. The Duc de Longueville, on his return from Normandy, went to St. Germain to pay his respects to the Queen, and the Duchess felt that she could no longer refrain from doing as much. But she did it in her own haughty fashion, appointing her own time, as if she had been a foreign sovereign, and keeping the Queen waiting, all of which did not lessen her Majesty's dislike to her. When she actually found herself in the presence, both Madame de Motteville and the Duchesse de Nemours record that natural embarrassment prevailed and she became speechless.

In response to the clamours of the populace, who now longed for nothing but peace and goodwill, Condé at last brought the King and Court safely back to Paris, to the Palais Royal, where the Queen thanked him in these words :

'The service you have rendered the State is so great that the King and I should indeed be ungrateful if we could ever forget it.'

It is said that as he went away some one whispered in his ear, 'This is a greatness of service which makes me tremble for you.'

Shortly after the return of the Court the people of Paris desired to show their satisfaction at the event by giving a ball at the Hôtel de Ville to their Sovereign. In order to be away from the Court Madame de Longueville had withdrawn to Chantilly, much to the dismay of the Queen, who foresaw trouble when the intimacy of the members of the Condé family was thus visibly re-established. She desired to give expression to her hostility to the Duchess by not having her invited to the ball, but the latter was determined to be there. Condé himself had to interfere, as well as his mother; and Anne of Austria yielded at last, saying sarcastically, 'she was surprised that important Madame de Longueville had made such great efforts to obtain such a little thing.'

This small incident shows that Madame de Longueville was gradually making way with her brother, for whom Paul de Gondi also lay in wait. It was, likewise, an instance of the

small personal intrigues mixed up with the
political ones that were going on. The marriage chessboard of the time alone is most
bewildering. It is almost impossible to follow
the unions that were concluded, still less those
that were planned one day and given up the
next. There was Mademoiselle, the daughter
of Gaston, who was looking out for herself.
Condé and Madame de Longueville desired to
bring about a match between the sister of the
beloved Marthe du Vigean and the young Duc
de Richelieu, an event which, when it was
accomplished without her permission and in the
face of Mazarin's opposition, irritated the Queen
more against Anne-Geneviève than anything
else had done. The Duke wanted a husband
for his daughter, Mademoiselle de Longueville.
The Coadjutor had planned and was trying with
all his might to bring about a marriage between
the Prince de Conti and Mademoiselle de
Chevreuse, whom he had compromised to an
extent which was doubly scandalous in his
position. And then there were ' the nieces,'
the terrible Mancinis and Martinozzis, whose

future establishments were almost as much an affair of state as that of the King himself, and one of whom, Marie Mancini—oh, irony of fate! —very nearly prevented their uncle's master-stroke, the Spanish marriage of Louis XIV. Another of them was the cause of the final quarrel between Condé and Mazarin, which was so far-reaching in its disastrous consequences. Laure Mancini was engaged to the Duc de Mercœur, of the House of Vendôme. The Cardinal asked Monsieur le Prince to sign the contract. He excused himself on the ground that he was no relation, and added, ' besides, there is something I have to ask myself before I could do anything of the kind, and that is the government of Pont de l'Arche for Monsieur de Longueville.' This had been one of the evaded conditions of the Peace of Rueil. Pont de l'Arche was a fortified place in Normandy, and Mazarin was faithful to Richelieu's wise policy, in pursuance of which the governor of a province was never to govern a fortress situated within it. But the great Cardinal would have refused unhesitatingly to comply with

such a condition.   His successor had promised
meaning not to keep his word.   The quarrel
was patched up for the time being.   Mazarin
pretended to be very friendly and forgiving.
Condé unsuspectingly wrote a somewhat impru-
dent letter to him, promising his support.   This,
when shown to the Prince's own partisans, as
Mazarin of course took care that it should be,
caused even the latter to fall away from him
and to come to an understanding with the
Coadjutor.   A trivial Court incident, in which
Condé's recklessly impulsive partisanship indis-
posed the Queen, added to the tension.   All
the while he was being urged on by his sister
to secure what she was more anxious to obtain
than anything else, namely, Marsillac's great
object, the coveted 'honneurs du Louvre.'
These were the right to the 'tabouret' for
his wife, and the privilege of driving his coach
into the courtyard of the Royal palace, honours
to which, being only the son of a duke, he was
not entitled in his father's lifetime.   It may
here be said they were granted, but afterwards
revoked under the pressure of the indignation

of the rest of the *noblesse*. All these favours, on the granting of which Condé was induced to stake his position, wore out his credit at Court and destroyed his influence elsewhere. At last Mazarin actually organised a sham plot against Monsieur le Prince, whose object was to cause him to commit mistake after mistake; and in this the Minister completely succeeded. Condé was led on to prosecute Gondi, Beaufort, and the Councillor Broussel. It had all been carefully prepared between Mazarin and the Coadjutor, but at the last moment the latter regretted the intrigue, or, at all events, was willing to have gone back and brought the rest of the Frondeurs round to Condé. But he was singularly guileless, and incapable of understanding what was brewing round him. Looking neither to the right nor to the left, he walked straight into the trap so cleverly laid for him.[1]

On January 18, 1650, the Princess-Dowager

---

[1] Promesse de Fidélité remise par Mazarin au Prince de Condé deux jours avant son arrestation 16 janvier 1650 (*Bibliothèque Nationale*). Collection Dupuy, vol. 775, fol. 122.

was with the Queen, who pretended to be unwell. Condé came in, and they all exchanged a few words. It was the last time he ever saw his mother.

An hour afterwards, in the Council Chamber, he was arrested with his brother and the Duc de Longueville, and all three were conducted to Vincennes, where their imprisonment was to last a whole year.

It was, of course, impossible to justify such a measure as this. The Queen, knowing perfectly well that she and Mazarin were in the wrong, was most anxious to conciliate the Parliament, and particularly Mathieu Molé. An order was given to the magistrates to send a deputation to the Palais Royal ; but the right-minded old lawyer refused to be one of them. The Chancellor in the Queen's presence explained to the deputation the motives of the arrest of the Princes. A few days afterwards a ' letter from the King ' was read to the assembled Chambers of the Parliament, in which the supposed grievances against Condé, Conti, and the Duc de Longueville were set forth at great length, their increasing power and insolence being described as a danger to the State which would leave only the semblance of royal power to the King when he attained his majority.

' Finally, and to prevent any anxiety which might be roused by evilly disposed persons on the occasion of this just and necessary act, his Majesty was willing to repeat that he had no intention to do aught against the declaration of October 24, but intended, on the contrary, that the said declaration should remain in full force and be maintained on all its heads.'

It was the height of irony at the moment when its most conspicuous clause had been violated in the persons of the Princes.

Immediately after the arrest the Queen had sent an order to the Dowager Princesse de Condé, who had always been her intimate friend and faithful follower, to withdraw to Chantilly with her daughter-in-law, Madame la Princesse, and her grandson, the young Duc d'Enghien, who was now seven years old.

The Duchesse de Longueville had been summoned to the Palais Royal, where it was

intended she should be arrested. On hearing
the fatal news, she had rushed to her mother's
house to inform her of what had occurred and
consult with her as to what should be done. It
was here she received the royal message. But
she contrived to leave the Hôtel de Condé
unperceived, and to take refuge with her
staunch friend, the Princess Palatine. That
very remarkable woman, of whom Cardinal de
Retz said, ' I do not believe Queen Elizabeth
had a greater capacity for directing a State,'
from this time forward played a great part in
Madame de Longueville's and her brothers' lives,
and proved herself the wisest and most reliable
adviser. On this occasion she hid Madame de
Longueville in a little house where Marsillac
and his brother-in-law joined her, and whose
windows she had to illuminate in honour of her
brothers' and husband's imprisonment, in order
not to let her presence be suspected by the
fickle population. The Frondeurs were delighted, and forthwith began to reappear at the
Palais Royal. The ignorant masses did not
realise that a mortal blow had been struck at

the very root of the principle for which they had fought and suffered.

All the nobles who had remained faithful to Condé left the Court. The Duc de Bouillon, who had attached himself to his person in a special manner, retired to Turenne in Auvergne. His brother, the Maréchal de Turenne, withdrew to Stenay, which was a fortified place, whose governor owed his post to Monsieur le Prince. His wife's father, the Maréchal de Brézé, went to Saumur ; and Marsillac, who had just become Duc de la Rochefoucauld by the death of his father, betook himself to his government of Poitou upon leaving Madame de Longueville. She herself made her way to Normandy in the coach of the Princess Palatine.

On her arrival at Rouen she was informed by the governor of the Citadel that, her husband being in prison, he could not, though much attached to her, do anything towards his deliverance, or that of her brothers, against the King, who was shortly to be expected in the province. She then turned to the Duchesse d'Aiguillon, Cardinal de Richelieu's niece, who governed Le Hâvre de Grâce for her ward and nephew, the young Duc de Richelieu, a privilege for which she was largely indebted to Condé. This lady had, however, had an interview with the Queen, and Mazarin had warned the young Duke that if he was tired of the tutelage of his aunt it would be much worse to be under the authority of Madame de Longueville, who by her cleverness always managed to get every soldier and every official unto her own side.   So she had to submit to another refusal. She next went to Dieppe, which was under the command of Montigny ; but neither prayers nor threats were of any avail, and he advised her to go to Flanders.   ' She knew,' says Madame de Motteville, ' that the greatest service she could render to the Princes was to keep Normandy for them.'   Therefore Anne-Geneviève would not give way.[1]   She used her utmost endeavours with the populace, the

---

[1] A Messieurs du Parlement de Normandie—Supplie humblement Anne de Bourbon, Duchesse de Longueville. . . . MS. Fr. 23044, fol. 54 (*Bibliothèque Nationale*).

officers and inhabitants of Dieppe, but they
sent their submission to the King. The Queen
now carried out her intention of bringing him
to Normandy, in the hope of thereby quelling
the revolt. The Cardinal had followed
Madame de Longueville with some troops
hastily collected. The Parliament of Rouen at
once assured the Queen of their fidelity ; the
Marquis de Beuvron, the governor, handed
over the Citadel, Pont de l'Arche and the
Castle of Caen surrendered. In Dieppe itself,
at the approach of the King's men the people
rose against Madame de Longueville. When
Plessy-Bellière, who was in command of the
royal troops, threatened to besiege the Castle
in which she had shut herself up, she left it by
a small back-door that had been forgotten and
was unguarded, followed by those of her women
who were brave enough to accompany her.
After walking six miles to a little fishing-
harbour, she found two small fishing-smacks.
In these she decided to embark, in order to get
to the ship which had been sent to meet her.
The wind was so high that the sailors advised

her not to make the attempt, and when she insisted on doing so the tide proved so strong that the man who tried to carry her into the boat dropped her, and she was very nearly drowned. Nothing daunted, she wished to proceed, but it proved impossible. Finally horses were procured. The Duchess and her attendants rode behind the men, and so in the middle of the night they reached the house of a gentleman of the Pays de Caux, who hid them and entertained them hospitably.

The following day a messenger was despatched to inquire for the ship which was waiting for Madame de Longueville. But it was then discovered that the skipper had been bribed by Mazarin, and if she had gone on board she would have been arrested. At last she succeeded in getting hold of an English captain, with whose assistance she reached Holland. Thence she went to Stenay, in Lorraine, one of the last remaining places that belonged to the House of Condé. Here she was joined by the Envoy of the Archduke, who had come to propose a treaty of alliance to her ;

and here also Turenne met her and the Ambassador at the head of his troops. The Duchesse de Longueville was now looked upon by Spain as the second power in the State, and, after her heroic wanderings for the sake of her brothers and her husband, the temptation to avail herself of this extraordinary position for their benefit was, no doubt, an overwhelming one. The document which was eventually signed by her and Turenne, and by Don Gabriel de Toledo, Envoy of the Archduke Leopold of Austria, brother to the Emperor Ferdinand III., contained the following clauses : [1]

That the war should be carried on jointly, in order to secure the liberation of the Princes and general peace. That the allies should not lay down their arms until this result had been attained.

That the King of Spain should furnish the Duchesse de Longueville and Monsieur de Turenne with 200,000 écus, to be employed in levying troops, plus 40,000 écus a month for

---

[1] 'Traité en original de Madame de Longueville et du Maréchal de Turenne avec Monsieur l'Archiduc Léopold.' Stenay, 30 avril, 1650. Vol. 3855, 19 Folios (*Bibliothèque Nationale*).

the paying of the said troops and for other expenses of the war ; and that, moreover, the King of Spain should allow the Duchesse de Longueville 60,000 raies a year for keeping up her house.

That 3,000 Spanish infantry and 2,000 cavalry, in the pay of the King of Spain, should be placed under the command of the Vicomte de Turenne.

That all fortified places conquered by him should remain, provisionally, in the power of Spain, but should be returned to France as soon as peace was definitely signed.

The Envoy had originally demanded the surrender of the city and citadel of Stenay ; but Madame de Longueville, while consenting to receive them there, would not give up the fortress, in which she continued to reside, and whence, with Turenne's assistance, she carried on a most active campaign, writing, negotiating, and rallying Condé's partisans round her and the Marshal. She remained in constant correspondence with the Princess Palatine, and the manifesto she caused to be printed at Brussels was issued by her from Stenay.

It began by giving an account of all the

persecutions to which her family and herself had been subjected, arising from the hatred of Cardinal Mazarin and his desire to make general peace impossible, and referred to the sufferings of the people which had resulted therefrom.

' The goodness of the Queen (she goes on to say) is blinded more than ever by the artifices of her Minister, and Monsieur le Duc d'Orléans, by his easygoing disposition, yields himself to the direction of this false Tribune of the people. Seeing, therefore, that I was the only person who retained the means of putting a stop to so many calamities, and that my conscience, my birth, and my duty powerfully compelled me thereunto, I moreover found myself urged on to undertake so great and glorious an enterprise by the prayers of the most notable persons in the Church, the army, and the law ('de l'Epée et de la Robe'), and by the supplications of the best inhabitants of Paris and of the principal cities of the Kingdom. But I feel especially fortified on this occasion by the affection, the counsel and assistance of Monsieur de Turenne, whose merit and valour are on a par with the highest enterprises, and who is as passionately devoted to the service of the King, the good of France, and the re-establishment of our House. . . ." '

She adds that during the minority of kings

the Princes of the Blood should be free to take care of the State. The King of Spain had therefore invited her to help him in the design he had formed to give peace to Christendom, concerning which he will not treat with Cardinal Mazarin, whereas he would willingly do so with the Princes. On this basis she and Monsieur de Turenne had treated with the Ministers of Spain, with the object of combining their forces, and promised not to lay down their arms until the Princes had been delivered.

All this time the other ladies of the family had been working for their common cause in their various ways. Madame la Princesse Douairière and her daughter-in-law, with the young Duc d'Enghien and the children of Madame de Longueville, had gone to Chantilly in accordance with the Queen's orders. Clémence de Maillé-Brézé had never, as yet, had any opportunity of showing the latent greatness of character that was in her, and the unloved wife of Condé had scarcely been taken into their confidence by the rest of the family. She now took advantage of the arrival of Lenet, the faithful adherent and counsellor of the House of Condé, whose memoirs[1] give the best account of what happened to all its members at this period in their lives, to speak her mind to him without reserve. She told him nothing would induce her to part with her son, and that no efforts and no dangers would be too great for her to brave in the service of her husband. Lenet grasped the situation at once. He foresaw that the alliance between the Frondeurs and 'the Mazarins' could not be a lasting one, and he had begun separate negotiations with both the Cardinal and the Coadjutor, ready to continue them with either, according to circumstances. He also knew that the position of the Princesses at Chantilly was not a very safe one. After receiving the confidences of Clémence de Maillé he made his plans, both with a view to carrying out her wishes and ensuring the safety of all, and laid them before Madame la Princesse and her mother-in-law. He proposed that the latter should go to Paris and personally implore the protection of Parliament for her

[1] *Mémoires de Monsieur Lenet* (1729).

H 2

sons and son-in-law, on the ground that the
Declaration of October 1648 had been violated
in their persons. During that time he himself
would conduct the young Princess, with her son,
to the south of France for the purpose of rousing
the population and placing her at the head of
a party which was to pursue the liberation of
the Princes by more vigorous means.

What he had expected very soon happened.
A gentleman-in-ordinary to the King arrived at
Chantilly, followed by troops, who remained at
a short distance from the house. His orders
were that the ladies and children should at once
withdraw to the Province of Berri. But he
was hoodwinked with the utmost cleverness by
the various persons concerned, and detained for
a week on one pretext and the other, whilst
Madame la Princesse and her son, with her
suite, rode across country to Montrond, where
they were safely encamped and in a position
to defend themselves before the stratagem was
discovered.

Although able to sustain a siege, the
Princesse de Condé wrote a dutiful letter to the

Queen, who chose to be amused at the adventure, and to take no serious steps in the matter.

The Dukes of Bouillon and La Rochefoucauld had gathered together the nobles, as well as the peasantry, in their vast domains in Angoumois and Limousin. In the last-named province was the Château de Turenne.

Facing once more the same dangers and difficulties as had attended her first journey across country, the young Princess went to meet them at the latter place, where she was enthusiastically received and fêted as long as she remained there. But the royal troops were approaching, and the struggle was too unequal. The castle was sacked, and the two Dukes barely succeeded in bringing Condé's brave wife and her child safely to Bordeaux. That city had had a parliamentarian Fronde of its own in 1649, when it was endeavouring to get rid of its hated Governor, the Duc d'Epernon, and the Prince de Condé had been its protector throughout, and had secured for Bordeaux, if not definite peace, at any rate a truce. The population was therefore inclined to receive

his family.   But when it became clear, through
her connection with the Dukes, that the
Princess represented direct opposition to the
King's authority, the Parliament raised difficulties and desired to close the gates.   However, the people carried the day.   Madame la
Princesse, once she had been authorised to
reside within the walls, became mistress of
the situation.   Throughout this difficult time
she displayed the greatest tact and moderation,
addressing the Parliament and the people
whenever necessary with rare felicity, although
this niece of Cardinal de Richelieu had only
learned to read and write a year after her
marriage.[1]   The actual power she was careful
to leave in the hands of the Dukes, who had
finally been admitted into the city, in spite of
the Sovereign Company's resistance.   Unfortunately, here again foreign interference was
countenanced, in direct opposition to the views
so frequently expressed by Condé himself.
Whilst the King's vanguard was approaching

[1] Arvède Barine, 'La Grande Mademoiselle.' *Revue des
Deux Mondes*, July 15, 1899.

Bordeaux, Watteville, the Envoy of Spain, was received in the town.[1] In the north the successful defence of Guise by Bridieu, against the Archduke and Turenne, drove the Spaniards back towards Brussels. But at Bordeaux the Spanish fleet was expected in the Gironde. The King and Court now started on their progress to Guyenne in order to endeavour to pacify that province, as they had pacified Normandy, and Mazarin committed the grave mistake of also sending the best troops to the south.

In consequence of this course of action Turenne, urged on by Madame de Longueville and in co-operation with the Archduke, to whom he practically dictated all his movements, was able to gain a series of advantages in the north, which culminated in the defeat of Marshal d'Hocquincourt at Fismes on August 26, 1650. The Dowager Princess had succeeded in escaping to Paris after the departure of her

[1] Traité fait entre Claire Clémence, Princesse de Condé, les Ducs de Bouillon, de la Rochefoucauld, etc. . . et Philippe IV. Roy d'Espagne, St. Sébastien, 26 juin 1650. Collection Dupuy, vol. 775, fol. 114 (*Bibliothèque Nationale*).

daughter-in-law, and caused much emotion by the appearance of one in her position, and so much respected, as a suppliant before the Parliament whose protection for her sons she had come to implore.[1]

'I nearly died of shame,' says Cardinal de Retz. But the sole result of this voluntary sacrifice of her pride to the good of her children was that she obtained leave to go and reside in the *château* of her cousin, the grasping Duchesse de Châtillon,[2] who shut out her friends and kept even her daughter-in-law at a distance. Here the proud and brilliant Charlotte Marguerite de Montmorency died on December 2, 1650, broken-hearted and almost forgotten, without having seen any of her family again, and without one ray of hope for the deliverance of those who were uppermost in her mind. Madame de Longueville received

[1] Requête de Charlotte Marguerite de Montmorency, Princesse Douairière de Condé, au Parlement en faveur de ses fils détenus à Vincennes 1650 (Minute), vol. 3855, fol. 31 (*Bibliothèque Nationale*).

[2] 'Testament de Charlotte Marguerite de Montmorency, Princesse de Condé de Chantilly, 9 août 1649.' Collection Dupuy, vol. 775, fol. 124 (*Bibliothèque Nationale*).

the news of this great blow at Stenay. When it reached her she wrote the following letter to the Reverend Mother Prioress of the Carmelites in Paris :

'Yesterday I received, at the same time, your three letters, of which the last informs me of our common loss. You can well judge of the state into which it has thrown me, and my silence, more than my words, must betoken my grief. I am overwhelmed, my dear Mother, and this blow finds me without strength in my soul. There are circumstances so cruel that it kills me to think of them, and yet I can think of nothing else. The poor Princess died in the midst of the affliction of her House, forsaken by all her children and attended only by the grief and torment which put an end to her miserable life. For it was the suffering of the spirit which brought about that of the body, and I think therefore that death harder than had she been killed by physical ills and tortures. She will leave everlasting sorrow in my mind, and is leaving it to such an extent that I can never feel happiness, even should any come to me, because my poor mother will never have shared in it before feeling the bitterness of her last hour. I know none of the particulars which accompanied it, and I apply to you, imploring you to let me know them accurately. It is only in lamenting myself that I can find relief.

Such an account would produce that sad effect, and that is why I ask it from you, for you can see that it cannot be rest which follows upon such grief as mine, but misery, hidden and endless. This I am prepared to bear in the sight of God and of my sins, which have laid a heavy hand upon me. He will perhaps accept the humiliation of my heart and the chains of my deep wretchedness. You will soften them somewhat if I can hope for that share in your friendship which belonged to her for whom we weep. That will be to me her most precious inheritance.'

The captivity of the Princes had been exceptionally rigorous, so that the health of the naturally delicate Prince de Conti and the spirits of the Duc de Longueville had suffered to a marked degree. Condé kept up a semblance of gaiety. To a certain extent, and in spite of all endeavours to prevent it, the prisoners were informed of what was going on. One day his physician found him watering a few carnations on the little terrace of the dungeon of Vincennes. ' Is it not strange,' he said, ' that my wife should be making war whilst I am looking after my garden ? ' He was sincerely grateful to that misjudged wife, but the expression of this feeling, for which she longed, was not allowed to reach her. On one occasion a messenger from the Queen Regent had been sent, for some purpose, to converse with Condé, and from him he endeavoured to glean information without showing his own ignorance.

'Your Highness,' said the man, 'should write to them who hold the command of Stenay to obey the King's orders.'

'A prisoner has no orders to give,' replied Louis de Bourbon ; 'and, besides, those who are at Stenay are not so unfaithful as to have any communications with the Spaniards.'

As long as he was not overborne by others, but acted up to his own judgment, it is to the credit and glory of the 'grand Condé' that he ever disapproved of and opposed anything which savoured of treachery to the King and country.

There had been various attempts to deliver the Princes.[1] In consequence, in the August of that year, they were transferred to Marcoussis, in the domain of Orléans, which pleased Gaston,

---

[1] *Mémoires de Jean-Hérault de Gourville* (1642–1698). Paris, 1724.

the King's uncle, who had full powers as Lieutenant-General of the Kingdom. Thus, on the one hand, the struggle turned on who should have Condé completely in his power, Mazarin or the Coadjutor and Beaufort, and the former had the better of it so far. Meanwhile things were not looking well for the Royal Army in the Bordelais. Everybody there was tired of the strife. The Parliament of Paris offered its good offices as mediator, and Mazarin made his peace with Bordeaux, whose deputies practically obtained all they wanted. Several articles, of no particular interest to the town, were settled amicably between the Cardinal in person and the Dukes of Bouillon and La Rochefoucauld. As Mazarin, who was very civil to both, drove them home from one of their meetings, he said : 'Who would have supposed a fortnight ago that we should be riding together in the same coach?' La Rochefoucauld's reply was the well-known saying: 'Monseigneur, everything happens in France.'

Madame la Princesse, who had been advised to go to Paris and implore the Queen's mercy

for her husband, was rebuked and treated somewhat coldly by her, and, having declined to
remain at Court or part from her son, she now
retired with him to Montrond, and thence continued to move heaven and earth on behalf of
Condé. But, after her partial submission to
the Queen, it was Madame de Longueville who
became the rallying point, as well as the guiding
spirit, of the whole movement on behalf of the
Princes all over France.

The war in the south being over, the Court
returned to Paris, but the Spaniards were advancing steadily in the north. Mazarin sent thither
the troops now set free in Guyenne, and, finding
that the Princes were no longer safe at Marcoussis, he extorted from the feeble Duc d'Orléans
his consent to their translation, on November 6,
to the Château du Hâvre, where they could
be and were more strictly guarded. Three
days before, he himself had been condemned by
Parliament to be hung in effigy in four different
places.[1] On December 15 the Spaniards and

[1] 'Que ledit Cardinal reconnu coupable du crime de lése-
majesté a été condamné d'être pendu en effigie. . . .' le 3 novembre 1650 (Imprimé) 4235, fol. ii. (*Bibliothèque Nationale*).

Turenne were beaten by Mazarin himself. But, on being recalled by the Queen, he now had to face the question of Condé's liberation, which had suddenly become a burning one. The Princess Palatine, always the friend of Condé and Madame de Longueville, and one of the cleverest diplomatists of her time, had been preparing the way for a solution by negotiating, secretly, with the Fronde and Mazarin at the same time. In January 1651 she informed the latter that, unless he decided to set the Princes free at once, she would enter into an engagement with the Coadjutor and the Frondeurs. But the Queen was violently opposed to such a course, and Mazarin's weakness, the peculiarly Italian method of securing an advantage by underhand dealings and procrastination, brought about his defeat. Anne de Gonzague concluded on January 30, with Gondi and his party, a general treaty and a series of personal treaties. The general treaty had for its object the deliverance of the Princes and the dismissal of Mazarin, to be replaced by Condé and the Duc d'Orléans alone. The personal treaties included clauses deciding on the marriage of the young Duc d'Enghien, aged seven, and a daughter of Monsieur (the Duc d'Orléans) aged three, and that of the Prince de Conti and Mademoiselle de Chevreuse. The Coadjutor was to receive a Cardinal's hat, Châteauneuf to be made first Minister of the Crown, and innumerable money gifts were to be secured to various important persons. All resistance having now become useless, the Cardinal sent an emissary to negotiate with Condé. He hoped that Anne of Austria would have joined him at St. Germain, but she was surrounded and practically kept a prisoner by the nobles and by the people of Paris, who were now asking loudly for the return of Condé and Madame de Longueville. All that the Queen could do was to inform him that on January 10 she had been compelled to sign an order for the release of the Princes. Mazarin hastened to Le Hâvre, where he arrived before La Rochefoucauld and the other friends of Monsieur le Prince, who were the bearers of the welcome news. With what grace he might he endeavoured to make his peace by persuading

Condé that he had not been the main instrument of his incarceration. Escorting the Princes
to the coach which was waiting for them, he
bowed very low to Condé, and could hear, as
they drove away, the peals of laughter which
responded to his sudden humility. He himself
went into exile, whilst the Princes, on reaching
Paris, were received with a semblance of
cordiality by the Queen and Court, with bon-
fires by the populace, who had lit them as
readily to celebrate Condé's imprisonment, and,
as partisans of their own, by the Coadjutor,
Beaufort, and their party, who had all along
been conspiring against him.

A few days later, on February 25, 1651, by
a Royal Ordinance, which was confirmed, with
much applause, by the Parliament in a plenary
sitting on the 27th, the innocence of the Princes
was proclaimed, and they were reinstated in
their respective governments.

So ended the first part of the Fronde, the
only one which it is possible, if not to justify,
at any rate to explain and even to excuse. No
better word than Condé's own can be used to

qualify not only his action, but that of all those who led and took any part in the deplorable internecine war which was called 'the New Fronde :' 'I went to prison an innocent person. I came out the guiltiest of men.'

CHAPTER III

THE SECOND FRONDE

MADAME DE LONGUEVILLE did not witness the triumphal entry into Paris of her brothers and her husband. She had remained at Stenay for the purpose of winding up the negotiations with Spain now that the object of the alliance, the liberation of the Princes, was an accomplished fact. Though she had acted in cooperation with Turenne, it was to her the Spaniards had looked all along as being the real authority, the master-mind of the party and the person on whose word implicit reliance could be placed. Condé was most anxious to free his sister and his friend as quickly as possible from the engagements into which they had entered. He and the Prince de Conti, as well as the Duc de Longueville, were therefore pressing her to return to Paris at once. The following letter,[1] written to Monsieur le Prince on February 24, 1651, shows the view she took of what it was her duty to do in the circumstances :

'Gourville will tell you why I cannot start on Monday, as my letters conveyed to you, and the reasons which compel me to await the reply of the Spaniards before setting out on my journey. I persuade myself that you will not disapprove of them, and that you will procure for us, as rapidly as you can, a suspension of arms on the Meuse, which will be the thing of all others that will justify my journey most, that will please Monsieur de Turenne best, and will give me the greatest confidence with the Spaniards. I no longer entreat you to do so after Gourville shall have told you the reason, as you will understand the necessity of the thing better yourself than I could show it to you. Good-bye, my very dear brother. I am dying to see you and to assure you that I am yours more than my own.

'Monsieur de Turenne, who is here, asks me to convey most courteous messages to you, and I myself tell you that he is finishing the affair as he began it, that is with feelings and in a manner so obliging towards you that I

[1] Published for the first time in the *Histoire des Princes de Condé*, by the Duc d'Aumale.

think I ought to apprise you of it, knowing such news will not be displeasing to you.'

On March 7, Madame de Longueville nevertheless yielded to the arguments of her family, and left Stenay before her task there had been fully accomplished. At Châlons-sur-Marne she was met by her brother Conti, and on the 13th she made her entry into Paris, where she was received with every mark of that universal admiration which had been won for her by her great ability, her magnificent courage, and her brilliant success.

She was immediately visited by Monsieur, accompanied by Mademoiselle, in great state, and on the same day was most graciously received by the King and Queen. Trusted and admired by Spain, feared by the Court, and the pride of her House, Anne-Geneviève de Bourbon was now at the zenith of her career.

Condé himself was at that moment the most powerful person in France. He had undertaken to bring to a close the negotiations with Spain, and so to release Turenne from the responsibility, which had now begun to weigh heavily on him. As Madame de Longueville had foreseen, hitches began to occur the moment she was no longer on the spot, and, although the citadel retained its little French garrison, the Spaniards refused to evacuate Stenay, which there had been every reason for hoping that they would do. The fact of Condé having had to take over these difficulties, for which he was certainly not responsible, was afterwards made use of against him, and both contemporary and later historians have insinuated that Monsieur le Prince was, even then, guilty of secret transactions with the foreigner, whereas his sole desire was, at that time, to disentangle the meshes in which his House and his party had become involved.

His next care was for the reception of his wife, who left Montrond on March 18, and to whom he wished to give every outward mark of his gratitude for her splendid conduct during his imprisonment. All this was carried out with great magnificence and display, amidst general sympathy and applause. In fact, the Prince himself and his House were, to all appearances, as powerful as they had been before his captivity, and the situation was the same in more respects than one, for he was again the person of whom every one asked favours and through whom everybody expected to get redress for their grievances. As usual, he undertook and tried to do more than was humanly possible.

Everything at this juncture turned upon the way in which the House of Condé would maintain its good relations with the Fronde. The present state of affairs existed thanks to the skill of the Princess Palatine, who had been inspired and directed at a distance by Madame de Longueville, and had succeeded in inducing that other still more powerful negotiator, the Duchesse de Chevreuse, to act with her. The Fronde had been led on to desire nothing so much as to have for their chief, together with the Duc d'Orléans as figure-head, the hero whose name was most likely to shed a reflected glory on their cause. The plan conceived by the two Ladies was to form a new league of the whole aristocracy under those

two leaders, and, by combining the influence
and interests of themselves and all their
followers, to build up an irresistibly strong
party, which in its turn should be able to supply
a strong government of its own, and so keep
out for ever Mazarin and all his works. The
basis and outward expression of this project
was the matrimonial clause in the 'general
treaty,' viz. the union, in the future, of the
children of Monsieur and the Prince de Condé
and the immediate marriage of the Prince de
Conti to Mademoiselle de Chevreuse. The
last-mentioned condition was the factor on
which now hung the whole situation, and its
prompt and unhesitating fulfilment was the
most imperative duty of every member of the
House of Condé and of all their sincere
partisans. Monsieur le Prince, as well as
Madame de Longueville, to whom the project
had been submitted at Stenay, had frankly
agreed to it at the time, and the latter, writing
to the Princess Palatine on November 26, 1650,
said, with reference to that matter, ' it is therefore to this we must hold fast.' Had that

course been adopted, the co-operation of Madame
de Chevreuse and of the Coadjutor would have
been secured once for all, this particular consideration being, for excellent reasons, uppermost in both their minds. The desired
marriage would even have induced Paul de
Gondi to wait more patiently for that Cardinal's
hat which was the one object of his personal
desire, because it represented to his extreme,
though carefully concealed, ambition the road
to power and the possible successorship to
Mazarin. Already during the first part of the
Fronde this question had been the cause of
endless difficulties. It will be remembered
that the Prince de Conti had been destined for
the Church, on account of his bad health (he
was even slightly deformed). In fact, he was
still, nominally, an 'ecclesiastic,' although of
course neither priest nor deacon, and when a
nomination fell in to France he and Madame de
Longueville had put forward his claim to be
made a Cardinal with great energy as against
that of the Coadjutor. The matter had been
settled by the Princess Palatine, through the

mediation of her sister, Marie de Gonzague, Queen of Poland, who caused one of the rival candidates to be accepted as the nominee of that country. So far, however, no practical result had followed from these various arrangements, which existed on paper only, and Paul de Gondi was growing dangerously restive and impatient under the delays in the performance of both the main conditions of the treaties.

The Queen was, of course, doing all in her power to injure Condé without appearing to do so, and to pave the way for the eventual return of the Minister, who, while absent in the body, was the guiding spirit of her every act, directing her policy, day by day, in its minutest details. On April 15 she suddenly deprived Châteauneuf of the seals, and gave them to Mathieu Molé, calling Chavigny back to her council at the same time. Without any justification the Coadjutor, Madame de Chevreuse, Monsieur, and everybody else, blamed Condé for a change with which he had had nothing whatever to do.

The storm was brewing, and the only way

in which it could have been averted was by
hastening the Conti marriage.   Instead of that,
the fatal mistake was made which practically
settled the fate of Monsieur le Prince and of
the Fronde.   The engagement was suddenly
broken off.   The whole affair has never been
entirely cleared up, and it is even now difficult
to know exactly at whose door the responsibility
for it should be laid.

M. le Duc d'Aumale suggests a very simple
but scarcely sufficient explanation.   According
to him, officious friends informed Condé of what
had been going on between Mademoiselle de
Chevreuse and the Coadjutor, whereupon he
burst in upon his brother, put the matter before
him, and, although the latter was very much in
love with his *fiancée*, then and there compelled
him to give her up.   But three of the greatest
families in France—the Lorraines, the Luynes,
and the Rohans—to each of which Madame de
Chevreuse was allied, could not have been
insulted in the person of her daughter, with
such a light heart, by even so reckless and
impulsive a person as Louis de Bourbon.

It seems pretty evident that the fateful breach was a deep-laid scheme, devised by the Queen and Cardinal for dividing the party at a single blow. In this they were perfectly successful. The evidence contained in Madame de Motteville's memoirs is really conclusive on that point, and this is how she relates the end of that unfortunate episode. Anne of Austria, 'caused Madame de Chevreuse to be informed that she did not wish this marriage to take place, as it had been planned in view of objects that were contrary to the service of the King. This order was the cause that all these proposals vanished and were spoken of no more.'

This, however, took place after the Queen had, somehow, won over Condé to the line she desired he should take up. The question is, how did she accomplish this and how was it that Madame de Longueville lent her hand to such a proceeding? The following is the account of public opinion on the subject and of the real facts, according to his view of them, which are given, in his memoirs, by La Rochefoucauld, who is generally to be trusted where his own interests are not concerned. He said of the Fronde that, seeing the marriage they were anxious to hasten continually postponed, they 'suspected Madame de Longueville and the Duc de La Rochefoucauld of having designs to break it off, lest the Prince de Conti should pass out of their hands into those of Madame de Chevreuse and the Coadjutor.' The true explanation of the delays is, according to him, the fact that Monsieur le Prince, 'having as yet neither concluded nor broken off his treaty with the Queen, and having been informed that the Keeper of the Seals, Châteauneuf, was to be sent away, wished to wait for the event, in order to let the marriage take place if Cardinal Mazarin should be ruined by Monsieur de Châteauneuf, or break it off and thereby pay his court to the Queen if Monsieur de Châteauneuf were driven away by the Cardinal.'

If this not very creditable explanation is the true one, it only shows how well Mazarin had succeeded in dragging Condé into a region of underhand diplomacy and intrigue, in which he was out of his element and invariably blundered in the most hopeless manner. Whatever the cause, the result was a complete breakdown of the entire edifice built up with so much skill and foresight by the Princess Palatine and Madame de Longueville herself. One of the immediate and serious consequences was the alienation of that faithful friend of the Condé family. The fierce resentment of Madame de Chevreuse [1] and of the Coadjutor was of course the most dangerous result, and, through them, the breach between Condé and the old Fronde soon became an accomplished fact. He himself, as far as he was capable of conceiving a plan and adhering to it, off the battlefield, desired to form a new Fronde in opposition to the old party. Both he and his sister had at that time an exaggerated idea of the power and prestige of their House, which, unbeknown to them, were really on the wane. Her step-daughter describes, with the bias to be expected in a person of her malevolent dis-

[1] August 9, 1651, M. M. to M. F. (Record Office. Foreign: France 247, No. 11).

position, the hauteur with which Madame de Longueville behaved at that time, and there is no doubt the 'natural majesty' her contemporaries frequently refer to with admiration could make itself felt 'objectionably' on occasions, although in ordinary everyday life her winning gentleness and simplicity were so conspicuous.

The Queen's latest policy, at the Cardinal's bidding, had been to flatter the Coadjutor and hold out hopes that she herself would procure for him both the Cardinal's hat and the high office of Mazarin. It is hardly possible to question the fact that he actually proposed to her to compass the assassination of Condé. We have Madame de Motteville's authority for it that Anne of Austria indignantly rejected the suggestion. But it seems highly probable that the idea of re-arresting him approved itself to her. It was also her Minister who induced the Queen to welcome the advances of that most dangerous foe, Madame de Chevreuse.

The influence of La Rochefoucauld, which might have been exercised beneficially just then, was *nil*, both on account of his perpetual vacil-

lation and because the Queen had succeeded
in lessening his ardour for the cause by giving
him back his government of Poitou before the
deliverance of the Princes. To this she had
added the promise to let him have the strong-
hold of Blay, which Condé had persistently
claimed for him. This promise was never
intended to be kept. He had, however,
actually granted him, for his son Marsillac, the
reversion of his government of Poitou. This
proves conclusively, if proof were needed, the
fallacy of the theory that La Rochefoucauld
was drawn into the Fronde by his love for
Madame de Longueville. His ardour for the
fray began to cool down the moment the main
object of his personal greed and ambition had
been attained, or nearly so. What he did not
appreciate was that, after the way in which he
had mixed himself up with the movement, it was
as fatal to his fortune as to his dignity not to
stand by his guns. For the present, he had not
yet actually admitted to himself any intention of
leaving them, and he was much taken up with
plots and counter-plots against the life of Paul

de Gondi and against his own. The actual
crisis was brought on by the following incident.
One night Condé was fetched out of bed by
what turned out to be a false alarm that troops
were approaching his house to arrest him. It
was the one thing in the world he dreaded, and
he instantly fled to his family seat of St. Maur,
near Vincennes. There he was joined at once
by a number of interested partisans, who wanted
to see what course he was likely to take and
how far they could turn it to their own advantage, and who were more or less disappointed to
find him, in his heart, still opposed to civil war.

The Prince de Conti meanwhile had tried
to explain his brother's conduct to the Parliament, but Mathieu Molé firmly and sadly
replied, ' This is but a melancholy preamble to
civil war.'

Louis de Bourbon now went to Paris and
endeavoured to come to an understanding with
the Duc d'Orléans. But their joint irresolu-
tion produced no result. Condé returned to
St. Maur, thoroughly discouraged and more uncertain than ever as to what he should do. But
he was soon joined by his sister, whose greater

decision of character and more constant partisanship caused her to urge him on to action.

On July 22 he yielded to her influence and signed the following treaty :

'We, the undersigned, declare that we persist in the will and intention we have of procuring the safety of the person of Monsieur le Prince, and of all those who will sign the present treaty, by all kinds of means, even by arms if necessary, and to let no occasion pass of taking them up until we shall have such certain assurances, with the avowal and consent of all, that we may have no further suspicion of designs against our persons.

'We moreover promise to listen to no proposals, nor to enter into any negotiation, without the express consent of the undersigned.

'And if it should so happen that it became necessary to take up arms they cannot be laid down unless each of the undersigned is satisfied in his interests, which he will declare on their being taken up.'

By the side of Condé's signature were those of Madame de Longueville, of their brother Armand de Bourbon, of the Duc de Nemours, the President Viole, and of La Rochefoucauld, in whose handwriting was the original. It was, to all intents and purposes, a declaration of war and a beginning of that disastrous and unpardonable combination, the 'Second Fronde.'

Nevertheless, although La Rochefoucauld had more to do with the drawing up of this fatal document than any one else, he now persuaded Condé to consent to his trying further negotiations before actually going to war. It was much too late to do any good, and Madame de Longueville strenuously opposed a policy of feeble dilatoriness, for, whatever her faults and the blame attaching to her in these transactions, she was never wanting in the courage of her opinions or of her actions. But her brother was strongly inclined to give way. She was hurt by La Rochefoucauld's unwillingness to comply with her wishes and by that growing indifference towards the cause which was so unchivalrous in her eyes and so unexpected, for as yet she understood the meaner sides of his character too little to fathom his true motives. But she acted on his suggestion that she should accompany her sister-in-law to Berri for a time, and let events take their course, because she saw it to be a sensible one and because it tallied with her own strong wish to withdraw as far as possible from Normandy and from her husband. Her position towards him had, quite lately, become a difficult one, because, in order to injure her, Paul de Gondi had enlightened the Duke on the subject of her relations with La Rochefoucauld.

After his imprisonment Monsieur de Longueville had become very cold towards the Fronde, with which he had associated himself willingly enough at first. So he gradually took up a neutral attitude between the party and the Court, which compromised him with neither, and eventually retired to the province of which he was Governor, and where his daughter, having him all to herself, did her best to increase his irritation against his wife. He now loudly and imperiously insisted on her joining him in Normandy, than which there was nothing she dreaded more. In fact, at that moment there was a tragic affinity between the feelings of the brother and sister. Both were in mortal fear of what to each would have seemed far worse than death, namely, the loss of their liberty, incarceration at Vincennes for the one, virtual imprisonment in her husband's castle for the other. They chose a bad way of escape, but their respective positions accounted for much of the wrong of which they were guilty.

When Madame de Longueville received her husband's summons she assigned, as a reason for her refusal to comply with it, the impossibility of leaving Condé in so difficult a predicament. When she accompanied Madame la Princesse as far as Bourges she took with her the eldest of her two boys, the younger one not being old or strong enough for such a journey. But the Duke at once demanded that his eldest son should be sent to him, and did so in language so threatening that his wife dared not resist him. Finding herself thus free from any responsibility, she went into retreat, at Bourges, in the convent of the Carmelites, to whose order she had always remained attached. This somewhat reassured the Queen, who was more afraid of her than of any other member of the hated House of Condé, and she became more conciliatory. In his sister's absence

Monsieur le Prince also decided to visit the King. But whenever he made any attempt at a *rapprochement* something invariably happened to mar the effect and indispose the Court. The time when the King would attain his majority and hold the intended *Lit de Justice* was at hand. On August 17, a Royal Declaration enumerated the grievances of the Crown. Condé immediately replied by one of his own, in which he protested against 'the imputations of his enemies contained in the rescript the King has issued,' and the contest went on. As for the Duc d'Orléans, one is scarcely surprised to find that he ran away from a complicated situation and retired into the country 'for rest and quietness.' On August 31 he had declared the Queen's favourable intentions towards Condé, at the very time when she and the Fronde concluded a secret treaty, devised by Mazarin, and based on a solid peace between himself and Madame de Chevreuse. On September 5, when nothing further concerning Monsieur le Prince was forthcoming on the part of the Court, a meeting of his supporters was convened by him at Chantilly, at which violent measures were under consideration, but no decision was arrived at. Condé now hastened to Trie, in Normandy, the residence of his brother-in-law, in order to ascertain how far he could depend on his support, but he found him committed quite as much to the Regent as to himself.

On September 7, when the young King solemnly repaired to the palace to hold his *Lit de Justice*, the Prince de Conti presented a letter from his brother explaining and apologising for his absence on so important an occasion. Louis XIV. handed it, unopened, to the Maréchal de Villeroy. The die was cast. The new reign had begun without Condé's taking his natural place by the side of his cousin and sovereign. In consequence of this act of over-undutifulness deserters from his cause became numerous. It was impossible to remain blind to that fact when, on September 9, at another meeting at Chantilly, it was seen how the number of those who assembled there had shrunk since the previous occasion.

Monsieur le Prince now proceeded southward, slowly and hesitatingly. He was followed by a royal messenger from Gaston, who proposed new terms on behalf of the Court, under his own guarantee, by way of a reply to the latest overtures of Louis de Bourbon But, by a series of involuntary, or more probably voluntary, mistakes, the messenger did not overtake him in time. On September 15, 1651, he reached Montrond, where he was met by his wife, his sister, and the Dukes. A last solemn deliberation took place. Condé himself still pleaded, though more feebly, his deep-rooted aversion to civil war in any form. At the same time, he knew his life and liberty to be in jeopardy, and that to rely on the Court was vain. Anne-Geneviève, Conti, and even La Rochefoucauld, urged him on to a breach. The casting vote was that of Madame de Longueville. Like her brother, she had everything at stake. But that was not her only motive ; far from it. She was much too clear-sighted not to appreciate her great brother's weakness wherever diplomacy and a cool head in the management of affairs were required. On the other hand, she knew him to be un- rivalled and in possession of all his greatest qualities on the battlefield, where he would find himself in his element. Her pride in him made her long to see him shine there, and carry everything before him once more.

When, at last, the hero of so many victories yielded to the counsels of his friends, and of the Duchess in particular, he said :

'You compel me to draw the sword. I shall be the last to replace it in the sheath, but you will weary of it soon enough, and you will forsake me.'

It was but too true of the others, but not even the thought of such faithlessness could ever have entered the fearless mind of the sister who shared with him every danger and every adversity she had largely contributed to bring- ing upon him, and who would never have any part in Court or any other favour so long as the same was not to be his.

As was to be expected, the moment *le grand Condé* had committed himself irrevocably, he began, with the utmost decision and the steadiest hand, to carry out his warlike plans. He left his wife, his son, and his sister in Berri under the protection of the Prince de Conti, the Duc de Nemours, President Viole, and another friend, Vineuil, to each of whom a distinct part and a distinct responsibility had been assigned by him. He himself, accompanied by La Rochefoucauld, proceeded to his new province of Guyenne, the government of which he had secured by means of an exchange, there to stir up the population, and if possible bring about a rising. To the Duc de Nemours had been entrusted the military command, for which he was perhaps less well fitted than Condé believed him to be. Charles Amédée de Savoie, the second of the three brothers who became, in succession, Dukes de Nemours, and of whom the youngest eventually married Marie d'Orléans, daughter of Monsieur de Longueville, was supposed to be one of the most fascinating men of his time. He had been passionately devoted to Madame de Châtillon, who preferred Condé, but without ever quite giving up her hold of Nemours.

He now fell in love with Madame de Longueville. She had always disliked the Duchesse de
Châtillon, between whom and herself there had
been a constant rivalry. This resulted in an
episode which it is not altogether easy to explain or to excuse, while its consequences were
unfortunately very far-reaching.

Anne-Geneviève de Bourbon was still as
irresistibly charming as ever, and her natural
coquetry had not been subdued, as it was so soon
to be. There is no sort of evidence to show
that there was any truth in the gross libels of
La Rochefoucauld, or that she ever seriously
cared for any one but himself. In all probability
there was between her and Nemours nothing
but a thoughtless flirtation, carried further than
was wise or dignified, and which began and
ended in her strong desire to bind him more
closely to her brother and his party. In fact,
the whole story only confirms, years after they
were written, Mazarin's shrewd remarks about
Madame de Longueville and the means by
which she tried to win friends and adherents
for Monsieur le Prince. But of course slander

got hold of the affair and distorted the facts, which, thus transformed, reached the ear of the Duc de La Rochefoucauld. To all appearances, it furnished him with what he wanted, namely, an excuse for a quarrel, which, with a woman of her type, was equivalent to a breach. In this way the great personal tragedy of her life was brought about. She had given her whole heart and mind to this man, and although we know the motives which, on his side, led to their *liaison*, it is impossible not to believe that he had become devoted to her as time went on. For three years they had been united by the closest friendship. They had fought for the same cause, shared the same dangers, and during their long separation, when Madame de Longueville was at Stenay and La Rochefoucauld carried on the war in the south, they had corresponded continually and most affectionately. But the master-passions of the author of the ' Maxims ' were vanity and ambition. For neither of these was any further satisfaction to be got out of the relationship, and his feelings for her, such as they were, had probably cooled

down by this time. So now, on the first pretext, without waiting for a personal explanation,
which would have set everything right, he
broke with her, with as much ostentation and
éclat as it was possible to give to such an event.
Indeed, as if this were not enough, he took
the meanest revenge in his power on the woman
to whom he owed so much by trying to turn
against her, first her brother, whom he knew to
be next to himself the object of her strongest
affection, and afterwards, as far as he could, all
the rest of the world. We have it on his own
authority that he insinuated to Condé that his
sister betrayed his interests for those of
Nemours, heinously hinting at the same time
that 'if a similar fancy took her for another
she was capable of going to the same extremities
if he desired it.' These words are recorded in
those brilliant and infamous 'Memoirs' which
were and are still such delightful reading.

Meanwhile Condé, on leaving Montrond
with La Rochefoucauld on September 16, had
betaken himself to Bordeaux, where, thanks to
the popularity he owed to his former interven-

tion on behalf of the province, he was received with great enthusiasm by the people and the Parliament. What he had come to accomplish was, however, a matter of great difficulty. An expedition was being sent against him under d'Harcourt, and Monsieur le Prince had neither troops nor money wherewith to get any. It would take too long to describe the expedients to which he was driven in order to procure both. But the end of it was that he entrusted to the Comte de Tavannes the difficult task of bringing right across France, from Stenay, his own old troops whom he himself had trained. As this was not sufficient, he also sent the Duc de Nemours to the Netherlands to secure a Spanish contingent, Lenet having previously gone to Madrid for the purpose of negotiating a treaty, framed very much on the lines of the one Madame de Longueville had concluded at Stenay, and which would ensure Spanish soldiers and subsidies. It was signed on November 6, 1651. By-and-by Watteville entered the Gironde with a Spanish flotilla of eight war-vessels, and at last, after a delay of many months, Condé opened the campaign, and opened it with a brilliant success. But the Comte d'Harcourt was now advancing upon him with an army of 15,000 men. Monsieur le Prince was in a position of marked inferiority, with nothing adequate to oppose to such forces except his name, which was a thing to conjure with. As was so constantly the case with Napoleon I., wherever he was not present in person something went wrong, and so loss followed upon loss.

In Paris, meanwhile, the face of things had changed. Châteauneuf had entered the Cabinet with an undertaking to recall Mazarin as soon as possible. But he filled his office so well and so successfully that the Cardinal was growing anxious for his own position, particularly since the new Minister, invoking many excuses, proposed one delay after another, in which Anne of Austria appeared quite willing to acquiesce. Suddenly, at the end of November 1651, Mazarin entered France with a little army under d'Hocquincourt. The King and Queen were at Poitiers, Châteauneuf having

considered a royal progress thither desirable
for the purpose of pacifying that part of the
country. It was there the Cardinal joined
them, and, after having been received most
cordially by both, took over the reins of
government in good earnest. This bold move,
which, from his own personal point of view,
had much to justify it, was to the advantage of
Condé, because it induced the ' Old Fronde ' to
rally round him as against the common enemy.
Madame de Chevreuse and her personal
friends alone adhered to the engagements she
had entered into, and, placed between Monsieur
le Prince and Mazarin, chose the latter once
for all. Paul de Gondi continued to play fast
and loose with both sides, lest, by taking up a
decided position, he should miss his Cardinal's
hat.

The Parliament of Paris was again put in
motion. A few months before it had registered
the decree proclaiming the Prince de Condé,
Madame de Longueville, Conti, and the Dukes,
rebels against the King. It was now persuaded
to issue an ordinance that this sentence should

not be carried out, and to renew all its old declarations against Mazarin.

The Duc d'Orléans, at whose disposal Condé had placed the contingent brought across from Flanders by Nemours, joined it to his own, which had been sent to the Loire to hold out against the Royal army, in spite of the disapproval of Monsieur le Prince, whom this arrangement effectually cramped in the south. The fatal blow, however, came in the shape of news that Turenne and his brother, the Duc de Bouillon, had definitely made their peace with the Court.

Turenne had long been tired of his false position of open resistance to the royal authority. At Stenay, as soon as the all-powerful influence of Madame de Longueville was removed, he began to show signs that he considered himself bound to the Fronde only so long as his pledges to Spain had not been redeemed. He had by now grown so weary of it all that he actually took the decisive step in spite of the fact that, shortly before, his brother had given his word to La Rochefoucauld that both would continue to follow the fortunes of Condé. In the circumstances, the latter resolved to go himself to the Loire and to Paris, and take the command of those of his own old troops who were under Nemours and Beaufort, in the hope that their achievements would, from a distance, influence the state of affairs in Guyenne. His friends, when consulted as to the wisdom of this plan, were undecided. But Madame de Longueville, with the Condé instinct for action and the rare quality of consistency, unhesitatingly advised him to do that which he felt to be right. Thereupon he determined to cross the lines of d'Harcourt, and appear suddenly in Paris. The command was left nominally to the Prince de Conti. But the real authority was to be in the hands of his sister, with whom his wife was to remain, and, under them, Lenet and the Comte de Marsin, one of Condé's favourite officers, were to have the management of all minor details. Together they were to form a provisional government and to keep Bordeaux in hand, with the help of Spain.

L

Monsieur le Prince hoped that these arrangements would prove adequate for about a year,
during which time he intended to achieve real
and decisive successes, at the centre of action,
in Paris and on the Loire.

At the end of March 1652, when his
preparations were complete, he started on this
bold but wisely conceived expedition, with his
usual pluck and buoyancy. He was accompanied only by La Rochefoucauld and his son,
the young Prince de Marsillac, besides two
other friends and a servant, and in the memoirs
of both the Duke and Gourville are to be found
most dramatic accounts of this adventurous
journey across country and the dangers they
encountered. When, at last, the little party
reached the gates of La Charité, Gourville was
despatched to inform the Duc d'Orléans that,
after joining their army, Monsieur le Prince
would come to Paris. But, of course, the
Court had already been warned of his movements, and he was being pursued. After a
hair-breadth escape, he safely reached the
château of the Duchess de Châtillon, the

object of his latest passion, and was informed
that his army was only a few miles off, so that
he was able to join it on April 1, 1652.

Taking the command at once from
Beaufort and Nemours, who were not of much
account in the eyes of the enemy, he changed
the face of things, and routed d'Hocquincourt
at Bléneau. Turenne was informed that all
was not going well with the army, and he came
immediately to the support of the Marshal,
against what he supposed to be an attack from
Nemours. One glance at the battlefield convinced him that he had been mistaken. 'Ah,'
he exclaimed, 'Monsieur le Prince has come!'
He withdrew to a better position after meeting
the bulk of the Royal troops, and before taking
the offensive. In his turn, on seeing the
masterly preparations that had been made,
Condé recognised the strategy and foresight of
his greatest pupil. In the combat which
ensued the two great rivals were face to face
for the first time, and the result was that
neither army could gain upon the other. One
retired towards Gien, the other to Châtillon,

where Condé left his troops under the command of the Comte de Tavannes, and, acting on the advice of Chavigny, started for Paris. The view of the latter was that the Prince would otherwise lose the support of Monsieur, who was on the point of being won over to the Court again by the Coadjutor.

The star of Mazarin was in the ascendant even with the people and the bourgeoisie, who longed for nothing but peace and the King's return. Condé, once he had ceased to follow the dictates of his own conscience and left the straight path of duty, was never certain of his own mind except in actual warfare. He therefore yielded to persuasion, and left another to deal with Turenne, which, in his present position, was a fatal mistake.

When he arrived in Paris, where all was in confusion, he tried to pacify the Duc d'Orléans by giving every one to understand that he was in favour of any concessions short of allowing Cardinal Mazarin to resume power. But, in spite of the courageous support of Mademoiselle and of the Duchess, Marguerite de

Lorraine, second wife of Gaston, there was nothing to be done with that ever uncertain personage, now under the influence of Cardinal de Retz—for Paul de Gondi had secured the object of his ambition, the Cardinal's hat, on February 19 of that year.

After endless negotiations, overtures were made to the Queen, Condé insisting only on the fulfilment of his promises to his friends and the departure of Mazarin. No result followed. At last the beautiful Madame de Châtillon tried the effect of her charms, and, for the double purpose of showing her power and injuring Madame de Longueville, threw her influence into the balance in favour of peace. With that twofold object she endeavoured to turn against the latter her brother and the Duc de Nemours, over whom she had cast her nets once more, and compelled him publicly to throw over Anne-Geneviève in the meanest way. In this noble enterprise she was joined and assisted by La Rochefoucauld. He tells us in his 'Memoirs' that he himself invented '*cette machine.*' That is what he calls the unworthy intrigue against

the woman for whom he had professed a
romantic and disinterested attachment, which
was intended to satisfy his vindictive feelings
and promote his selfish ends by securing a
profitable arrangement with the Court. To
arrive at this result he worked on the genuine
jealousy of Monsieur le Prince entertained by
Nemours, who was again as much in love with
Madame de Châtillon as ever, and induced the
former to get more and more entangled with
her. Condé was persuaded to present a kind
of ultimatum to the Queen, in which he declared
he would remain loyal to the Duc d'Orléans,
and, if the promises to his friends were kept,
he would be satisfied with ' the honour of having
worked for the general peace.' Of course,
La Rochefoucauld had a lion's share in the
advantages that had been promised to the head
of the party. For his brother Condé claimed
the government of Provence instead of that
of Champagne, for the future author of the
' Maxims ' the same rank as the Duc de
Bouillon and a sum of money large enough to
enable him to treat for the government of

Saintonge or Angoumois, or any other at his discretion, for the Duchesse de Châtillon 100,000 écus. The name of Madame de Longueville alone does not appear on the list, although it was she who had made the greatest sacrifices in the cause, and had even sold her jewels to satisfy her creditors. It was as ungrateful on the part of those who omitted it as the fact must be to her credit in the eyes of posterity. What this treaty was really intended to convey with regard to Mazarin's return it is difficult to make out, so contradictory are the terms that were used in drawing it up. In such circumstances the Cardinal was in no hurry to reply, and de Retz saw his opportunity of bringing about a definite breach between Condé and Monsieur, by which he himself could profit. During all this time his army, left in the command of Tavannes, was not doing well, and now a great misfortune happened to Louis de Bourbon. This was the treachery of Charles de Lorraine.[1] Through his sister, the Duchesse d'Orléans, he

---

[1] Letter of Charles de Lorraine, Coulommiers, June 19, 1652 (Record Office. Foreign : France 247, No. 14).

had signed a treaty with Gaston and Monsieur
le Prince in January 1652, and having at last
come to the assistance of their army he proceeded to negotiate with both sides, and finally
betrayed Condé in the face of Turenne's troops.
All was lost, and the Prince was left to regret
having yielded to interested advice instead of
the wise and steadfast counsel of his sister, his
only strong and reliable friend.

Too late he made a last heroic and desperate
but perfectly useless appeal to arms, and the
result was the deplorable fight, near the Porte
St. Antoine, on July 2, 1652, between the Royal
troops under Turenne and the divisions of
Nemours and Beaufort commanded by Condé.
Both armies were pressing forward into the
Place de la Bastille. Turenne had in his favour
an overwhelming superiority in numbers. When
it was discovered that the gates of Paris had
been closed against them, Condé and his
valiant little contingent, thus locked up in this
narrow space, were about to be cut to pieces.
Mazarin, from the height of Charonne, where
he was with the King, looked down upon the

unequal combat. Gaston had resorted to one of his usual devices. He was in bed, pretending to be ill, and devoutly hoping that Condé and his followers would be destroyed. His daughter alone had honour and courage and righteous indignation left in her, and ' la grande Mademoiselle ' obtained her contemptible father's signature to a paper which she so skilfully used that she succeeded in getting the gates opened for Condé and his followers. When this was done she ordered the cannon of the Bastille to be fired on the Royal army.

' That shot has killed her husband,' remarked Mazarin, for it was known to all that Marie-Louise desired to be Queen of France. She was as well aware of the consequences as the Cardinal, but she faced them. The same shot settled the fortune of the day. The coach which was to have driven Condé to prison brought the King back to his mother. Nemours and La Rochefoucauld were severely wounded, but Monsieur le Prince was unhurt, and he, as Mademoiselle tells us in her memoirs, thought only of his friends and of his country.

The remainder of that month was spent in useless deliberations. There were revo-lutionary scenes at the Hôtel-de-Ville. Parlia-ment declared the Duc d'Orléans Lieutenant-General, once more, in spite of the majority of the King, who was described as being 'the prisoner of Cardinal Mazarin,' the Prince de Condé Generalissimo, and the Duc de Beaufort Governor of Paris. These decisions were communicated to the various Parliaments of the other cities of France. A few days afterwards it was decreed that, to provide for new levies of men, the remaining pictures and statues belong-ing to the Cardinal should be sold and the proceeds added to the sum previously realised by the sale of his great library. All this lowered the Fronde more and more in the eyes of right-minded people.

On July 30 the ghastly duel between the Duc de Nemours and his brother-in-law, the Duc de Beaufort, in which the former fell mortally wounded, gave the party its deathblow. La Rochefoucauld declined to accept the post of Nemours, on the plea that his wounds compelled him to seek repose at home. Condé, deprived of one friend after another and no longer willing to listen to Madame de Longueville, was entirely in the hands of the Duchesse de Châtillon, who now urged him to rely altogether on that Spanish alliance which already weighed on him so heavily. Just then he fell seriously ill. All around there was but one clamour for the end of this senseless war.

Acting under the shrewd advice of Mazarin, the King proclaimed a general annesty for all those who had taken part in the events of the last few years and were willing to make their submission to the Crown. This wise measure finally dissolved the Fronde. But Condé's pride would not allow him to submit. A solution of all his difficulties was within his reach had he taken advantage of the new Edict to break with Spain and send away his troops. But, to his lasting misfortune, he chose the alternative of war, for which there was now no possible excuse, and, with his troops, left Paris, forsaken by every one. The magistrates entreated the King to return to his capital.

The burghers of Paris, under skilful leaders and with the connivance of the Court, took possession of the gates, and on October 21, 1652, the young Sovereign and his mother made their entry into their good city of Paris amid many rejoicings. The following day he held a *Lit de Justice* which restored all things to their former condition as far as the Parliament was concerned, and very soon order was permanently re-established. It was the decisive and well-merited victory of Mazarin, who, directing everything from afar, had left the Fronde to display its own incapacity, and had finally restored the Monarchy as the emblem of the nation in the sight of all men.

He himself, very prudently, kept out of the way for some time longer. But on February 3, 1653, his entry into Paris was a veritable triumph, and at the side of the Queen, his staunch friend, he found the two great diplomatists to whom he owed so much, Madame de Chevreuse and the Princess Palatine. With consummate wisdom, he took no vengeance of his enemies. Cardinal de Retz alone was

arrested as early as December 1652, and con-
fined at Vincennes for some time. This was
an indispensable precaution. La Rochefoucauld, without Madame de Longueville, had
ceased to be dangerous. He was allowed to
withdraw to his place in the country, without
having to invoke the benefit of the amnesty,
and to remain there, out of sight, for a few
years. When he was seen again in society all
had been forgotten, and in 1659, thanks to the
powerful Minister against whom he had fought
so strenuously, he began to enjoy a pension of
8,000 livres. It was by such methods that
Cardinal Mazarin consolidated his dearly
bought achievements.

The great and real sufferers, no doubt
deservedly so, were Condé and Madame de
Longueville. In some secret letters of the
Princess Palatine he is designated alternately
as 'the valiant one' and 'the uncertain one,'
and nobody knew or judged him better than
Anne de Gonzague. Like himself, his sister
was ever valiant, but with her there was no
uncertain purpose. From the very threshold

of these disastrous wars, she followed a perfectly straight line of conduct, never losing sight of the one object, and, given the original and unpardonable mistake, she acted ever after with wise foresight and unshaken firmness.

It will be remembered that she had been left behind at Bordeaux, virtually, though not nominally, in authority. The Prince de Conti, who had all the powers of a Governor of Guyenne, was assisted by a kind of Council of Regency, consisting of the Princess de Condé, Madame de Longueville, Marsin, Lenet, and President Viole. Louis de Bourbon's devoted wife had relapsed into that self-effacement which was natural to one of her retiring and unassuming disposition. The Prince de Conti, now 23 years old, was supposed to be still entirely under the influence of his sister, but her power over him was not what it had been. His weak nature placed him at the mercy of many other influences and many temptations, and he was just then intoxicated with the importance of his new position, and chafing under her tutelage. This state of things added to the difficulties of the situation in the absence of Monsieur le Prince.

Anne-Geneviève was a saddened woman at this time. The breach with La Rochefoucauld had been the greatest disappointment of her life. The knowledge that he was openly slandering her and trying to separate her from her favourite brother came upon her as a crushing blow. In the midst of all this trouble she received the intelligence of the tragic death of Nemours. The news from Paris became worse and worse. She herself fell ill. The only ray of sunshine was the faithful devotion of comparatively humble friends, the two Scudérys. Chapelain, the author of 'La Pucelle,' had written to express his concern at her illness, and when replying to his letter she asked him for the eighth volume of 'Le Grand Cyrus,' which was then coming out. When she received it she was profoundly touched to find that in the depth of her adversity and the disgrace of her party it had been dedicated to her. On the volume was her crowned initial' A.,' supported by an eagle and a ' Jupiter Tonans,' with the bold legend, 'Qui ne l'honore pas est digne de la foudre' (Him who does not honour her Jove's thunders shall destroy).

On August 29, 1652, Madame de Longueville wrote to Chapelain : [1]

'You will judge by my eagerness in asking you for the eighth part of " Cyrus " of the joy with which I received it. I confess, though, that it is not without shame I look upon the continued generosity of Monsieur and Mademoiselle de Scudéry ; for, although there is much pleasure in being its object, there is so little in letting the world believe that one does not deserve to be so, that this last thing prevents one's feeling the satisfaction the first would afford. . . . If ever I am able to show my gratitude to those two generous persons, I shall do so with extreme joy.'

Complications were thickening in Bordeaux. The most reliable supporter of the Duchess in the Council was President Viole, one of the members of the Paris Parliament. He was thoroughly devoted to the Fronde and to her, but Lenet, who was invariably in favour of compromise, contrived to get him recalled by Condé, and he himself entered more or less into the conspiracy formed against Madame de Longueville by La Rochefoucauld and the Duchess de Châtillon, in order to induce Monsieur le Prince to treat with Mazarin. Lenet did nothing openly hostile ; but, by keeping the conspirators informed of what was going on, he served them very effectually, and made the duties of Madame de Longueville more and more difficult to perform. The Comte de Marsin was a very able man and devoted to Condé, but a certain soldierly roughness prevented him from disguising his unwillingness to yield to the Prince de Conti. He became her only real support after the departure of President Viole. Marsin had been left in charge of all purely military matters, and he played his part so well and so successfully that he saved the situation in Guyenne, as far as was possible, in the absence of Monsieur le Prince.

The Comte d'Harcourt, greatly irritated by Mazarin's ingratitude towards himself, left the Royal army of which he was in command on July 10, and in face of this desertion Marsin

M

became very hopeful. But, almost simultane
ously, the Spaniards failed him by declining to
give any assistance in besieging Blaye unless
that town were given up to them. Therefore,
nothing could be done in that direction.
Nevertheless, he kept up the position until all
was lost in Paris and Condé himself was on the
way to Flanders. Mazarin now sent the Duc
de Candale, son of the hated Duc d'Epernon,
to take over d'Harcourt's command. He was
also to endeavour to conciliate the population
of Guyenne, and his double mission was successful.

Very soon the power of the Fronde was
entirely restricted to Bordeaux and a few neighbouring towns, and in that city itself discord
and faction reigned supreme. The principal
one was called *L'Ormée*, from its favourite
meeting-place, a little terrace on which grew a
number of elms, and it consisted of the dregs of
the population. Its number and power grew
to an alarming extent. Condé at a distance,
and Madame de Longueville on the spot, were
convinced of the importance of avoiding any

open conflict with these people. But La Rochefoucauld, among other libellous statements in the 'Memoirs,' declared that Madame de Longueville encouraged them in order to enhance her personal importance and make sure of some outside support for herself in her negotiations, both with the Court and with Condé. When he heard some of the insinuations of La Rochefoucauld, and wrote to Lenet on the subject, the latter had an explanation with the Prince de Conti concerning the favour supposed to be shown to the Ormée, and he states himself that the Duchess shed tears at the mere suggestion of a suspicion that she could be injuring her brother. Efforts were made to re-establish peace between the various factions at Bordeaux, but in vain. During a temporary absence from the town of the Prince de Conti, Madame la Princesse and her sister-in-law had to come out of the Archbishop's Palace, in which they resided, and rush into the midst of the crowd of armed men to stop the bloodshed. Madame de Longueville showed considerable firmness in dealing with the Ormée. Never-

theless its power continued to grow, and it
became a properly organised body, which, while
it supported Condé, was the terror of Parliament and of the Hôtel de Ville. After the
amnesty had been proclaimed it was the generally received opinion of the party of order that
he should not be upheld in his opposition to
the King. But the leaders of the faction
informed the Parliament that it would not be
allowed to register the Royal Declaration without having previously ascertained whether this
would suit Monsieur le Prince, who of course
pronounced against it and maintained that
Mazarin governed the country as much as
ever, although nominally in exile. Henceforth
there were only two parties in Bordeaux, one
for peace and one for war. The latter was, to
all intents and purposes, represented by *l'Ormée*,
so that, although in a minority, it was by far
the more compact and powerful of the two.
Unfortunately for himself, Condé's policy was
as mistaken as that which he had pursued in
Paris after the fight of the Porte Saint-Antoine.
He gave his representatives distinct orders to

ally themselves openly with the factious party, and, gradually gliding down the fatal slope, he again turned to Spain. This time it was with a view to inducing her to help him to obtain the assistance of England by treacherously appealing to her Huguenot sympathies.

Considering the state of public opinion on the other side of the Channel, and the irritation caused there by the shelter accorded to the family of Charles I. and the recognition of the Prince of Wales as King of England, he knew very well that it was only by betraying his religion, as well as his country, that there was any chance of his securing the co-operation of Cromwell and the Republican Government. Agents of Monsieur le Prince were sent to London to negotiate there, and afterwards to recruit soldiers in Ireland. Commercial and religious advantages were held out, mixed up in the usual way, and duly considered. Such things have been before and since. He despatched the Comte de Fiesque to Spain for the purpose of insisting on the complete carrying out of the treaty, and at the same time the city of Bordeaux, under pressure from the Ormée, sent deputies of her own to England, with powers to sign a treaty with Parliament, in order to secure troops and subsidies. Lenet preserved in his memoirs the full instructions accompanying the *plein pouvoir* which they received, dated April 4, 1653. A port on the Gironde, which she was to be at liberty to fortify, was actually offered to England. She would be free to attack La Rochelle and to besiege Blaye, and hopes were held out that, when the English appeared in the Gironde, the Protestants would unite with them. Indeed, a suggestion that Bordeaux might become a republic was thrown out. It was open treachery, and Condé countenanced it.

Fortunately the Huguenots, with the exception of a few isolated cases of individuals drawn into the meshes of the Ormée, showed no inclination to betray their country. They had long been granted every freedom in the exercise of their religion and complete equality in the distribution of State appointments, and their loyalty had been strengthened by Mazarin's wise and statesmanlike declaration of May 21,

1652, which confirmed all previous edicts of pacification. There is no doubt, however, that serious negotiations were entered upon in Flanders, in Cromwell's own name and with his authority, by his emissary[1] and Condé's friend, the Prince de Tarente,[2] offering Monsieur le Prince every assistance if he chose to place himself at the head of the French Protestants. But under pressure of these events Mazarin, with whom the Protector was also negotiating, hastened to recognise his authority and to assure him that, whilst continuing to afford shelter and protection to the Royal Family of England, France would do nothing to help to bring about the restoration of the Stuarts, a promise which was kept as long as Cromwell lived. The latter, in return, broke off in 1664 all negotiations with Condé and the Huguenots. Fortunately for the two great countries, two great statesmen presided over their destinies. Louis de Bourbon, being but the misguided chief

---

[1] Lieut. Colonel Sexby. See Gardiner's *History of the Commonwealth*, vol. ii. p. 90.
[2] *Mémoires du Prince de Tarente*, pp. 169-171.

of a petty faction, was unable to carry out his fatal plans.

We now come to the last phase in the slow death-struggle of the Fronde, the breaking up of the party of the Princes. Among other senseless and wicked charges brought by La Rochefoucauld against Madame de Longueville is the accusation that it was she who, by quarrelling with the Prince de Conti, brought on that consummation. In the first place, the Fronde was already hopelessly and irretrievably ruined by the far more serious causes which have been set forth in these pages. Secondly, the conduct of Armand de Bourbon was the result of his own weak nature and immature judgment alone. From the time when he first came to Paris and was thrown into daily contact with Madame de Longueville he had been under the spell of her great moral and intellectual superiority, and, besides, he undoubtedly found her personal charm more irresistible than is generally the case between brother and sister. This he showed in a manner that exposed them both to a certain amount of ridicule, and her enemies, headed by Mazarin for political, and La Rochefoucauld for personal reasons, took advantage of the fact to make her appear in the worst light.   Madame de Longueville's power over Conti began to wane directly after the Chevreuse marriage had been broken off, much to the young Prince's disappointment and displeasure.   It gradually ceased to exist during those long months at Bordeaux when he was surrounded by a little court of flatterers and drawn into a round of not very creditable occupations and amusements.   Interested friends and *protégés* of his endeavoured only too successfully to make mischief between the brother and sister, and, through Lenet, Condé was persuaded to believe their version of the stories, to which La Rochefoucauld gave shape.   They also represented to Armand that his brother had never shown any concern for his affairs, whereas in fact he had never left off demanding for Conti the important government of Provence, and had invariably watched over his interests in every possible way.   Finally, they insinuated that there was something absurd about his feelings

for his sister when, without his knowledge, La
Rochefoucauld had been her lover for years,
and she had begun an intrigue with the Duc de
Nemours, whilst she might at any moment
choose a new favourite from among her numerous admirers.   After this there were violent
scenes of anger and jealousy, which Madame de
Longueville found it a hard task to endure with
patience.   At first she succeeded in soothing
him by kindness and affection.   But one quarrel
followed another, and he put himself more and
more hopelessly in the wrong.   His unscrupulous courtiers had no difficulty in causing him
to become involved in an intrigue with a lady
of doubtful reputation, and at last his almoner,
a clever Gascon priest, the Abbé de Cosnac,
who saw clearly enough the way things were
drifting, determined to get a hold on this vain
and feeble youth and to secure him for the
Court and Mazarin, in order to make him serve
his own fortune.   Through a creature of his, he
very adroitly so conducted affairs that Conti
was led to negotiate with Spain and to fail in
what he was trying to obtain, after which Cosnac

pointed out to him the hopelessness of relying on the alliance. 'This blow,' says the Abbé,[1] 'which I administered skilfully enough not to arouse suspicion, is certainly what contributed most to the Peace of Bordeaux.'

To strengthen the impression thus produced, a somewhat violent popular outbreak followed in the city, during which the Prince himself ran some slight danger. Cosnac again pointed the moral, and, this time without much difficulty, induced Conti to enter into negotiations with the Court, and thus to betray the brother whose Lieutenant-General he was, just before the inevitable break-up of his party.

Madame de Longueville, who had been constantly accused of betraying his interests, remained staunch and faithful to Condé although he had ceased to treat her with any confidence or consideration. She felt how much she was to blame for all that had happened and the wrong he had done, and with him she would bear the consequences.

All the intrigues that were going on were

[1] *Mémoires de Cosnac.*

kept a dead secret from her. 'For,' says the Abbé de Cosnac, ' Madame de Longueville was so much attached to her brother's interests that she could never have consented to any treaty of peace in which he did not participate.' Conti still gave himself the appearance of being perfectly loyal and attentive to the Ormée. She was kept in absolute ignorance of the treachery that was in preparation, and the evidence of the almoner is absolutely conclusive as to her attitude throughout. She neither consented to any compromise nor did she condescend, for her own interest, to countenance the Prince's scandalous private life in order to bring about a personal reconciliation.

The Fronde, as was now inevitable, continued its downward career. A Royal Decree had transferred the Parliament of Bordeaux to Agen, and on March 3, 1653, the sittings of as many of its members as had obeyed the law were opened in that town. There were not councillors enough left at Bordeaux to dispense justice. One of those who had remained on the spot, named Massiot, determined to shake off the Ormée, and led a grand demonstration against them, after which courageous act his life was saved with some difficulty, and, at last, he also left for Agen. The same evening all the principal members of Condé's party met in the rooms of Madame de Longueville, and took the resolution never to separate from Monsieur le Prince, to get rid of all doubtful partisans, and to lean firmly on the Ormée.

Three days afterwards the Prince de Conti, at the Hôtel de Ville, signed a solemn treaty with that turbulent party. This was in accordance with Condé's instructions, which, at this time, were exactly like those of an officer giving military orders, regardless of all but the means to an end. To gain the day he ruthlessly sacrificed old friends and every other consideration. Lenet was instructed not to mix up the Prince's name with any acts of violence, but to leave the whole responsibility for them to his brother and sister, so that, later on, things might be the more easily put right and forgotten. The consequence was, of course, that the odium of whatever had to be done fell on

Madame de Longueville, whose firmness and strong character marked her out as the one responsible person.   Hence it came about that she was the chosen victim of the unknown per-petrators of an abominable vengeance, which took the shape of libellous and scandalous placards, put up regularly every night on the walls of Bordeaux, and attacking her most cruelly where she was most vulnerable.   These papers used to be taken down in the morning and burned by the hangman's hand, but the shameful practice could not be stopped, and the poor woman was systematically tortured in this way for many weeks.

Thanks to Mazarin's wise dealings with the Church, her representatives were now also tak-ing up the cause of Royalty.   The Bishops issued appeals in favour of the authority of the Sovereign, and, finally, the Archbishop of Bordeaux, Henry de Béthune, launched an excommunication against all those who, after the Amnesty, persisted in their refusal to submit to the King.   Preachers who condemned civil war were, it is true, fiercely attacked by the Ormée, but the movement continued in spite of all. A Franciscan, Father Berthaud, who was a very clever and fearless conspirator, did more than any one else to accelerate it. He received from the Court full powers to act with a view to promoting peace. Reaching Bordeaux in December 1652, he was helped and sheltered by Father Ithier, the Prior of the Franciscan convent there. The Prince de Conti was informed of what his real mission was. He accordingly sent for him and promised to protect him against the Ormée if he confessed the truth. But his great presence of mind enabled the friar, whilst admitting some things, to deny others, and thus to impress the Prince. Lenet tried to use him as an instrument to secure a peace in which Monsieur le Prince should have a part, and to induce him to write to the Court to the effect that Condé was still invincible, that he longed for peace, but would only accede to its being made if it were a general one, and therefore such as would satisfy Spain. Father Berthaud prolonged the negotiations as much as possible, until he was warned not to trust

Conti, after which he made his escape to Blaye.
The Prince and Lenet put a price on his head,
but he remained in hiding till February 11.
He then went to Paris and proposed to Mazarin
a well-thought-out and conciliatory plan, which
met with the latter's approval.   On his return to
Guyenne he managed to enter Bordeaux once
or twice in disguise, and to keep up communi-
cation with the town.   Father Ithier, meanwhile,
complained in public of having been deceived
by him, and continued ostentatiously his relations with the Prince de Conti and Madame de
Longueville, who thought very highly of him.
The business of their respective monasteries
had caused him to be in correspondence with the
Mother Superior of a neighbouring Carmelite
convent.   One of the inmates was the sister of
a man named Villars, who was among the
leaders of the Ormée and heartily tired of his
party.   Through her instrumentality a regular
treaty between the Court and her brother was
secured.   He intended so to arrange matters as
to let the Ormée destroy itself.   Others were
won over, here and there, and a complete con-

spiracy was in preparation which should have been ready to act, in Marsin's absence, on March 23. But at the last moment Villars's heart failed him, and he revealed everything to the Prince de Conti. General indignation was felt against Father Ithier. Armand de Bourbon, who himself meant treachery, had to make the greatest display of anger, and even Madame de Longueville and Cosnac were in favour of punishing him severely. It was, however, decided that they should pretend to know nothing. Father Berthaud came into Bordeaux once more, and was talking to Father Ithier, when the Prior was sent for by Madame de Longueville. His friend vainly endeavoured to persuade him not to obey the summons, and, upon his reaching her residence, he was arrested and placed before a commission, to whom, in the end, he confessed everything, even naming his accomplices. Among them was found to be the Carmelite nun, much to the distress of the Duchess, who would not allow her name to appear in the *procès-verbal,* and saved the convent from all the consequences of the part it had

taken in the affair. Father Berthaud had cleverly
made his escape.   The other conspirators were
fiercely pursued.   But Madame de Longueville
constantly tried to soften the inevitable severity
of the reprisals and to rescue whomsoever she
could.   Father Ithier was the chosen victim of
the hatred of the Ormée, who desired to tear
him to pieces, and it was only through her
intervention that he was spared a most terrible
death, and, instead, condemned to imprisonment
for life, from which he was released when all was
over.   He had been dragged and hooted all over
the town by the infuriated mob, all of which he
bore with the greatest dignity, and at last he was
deprived of his religious habit.   The Duchess
caused this to be restored to him, well knowing
there could be no greater consolation for the
poor priest, and all this merciful interposition of
hers very nearly caused a real sedition among
the Ormée.   Another courageous effort to shake
off its tyranny was made by a former officer
called Filhot.   He also was betrayed to the
Prince de Conti, and, unwilling to expose his
family to any danger, he threw himself into the

fray to protect them. Conti gave orders that
he should be taken, dead or alive. His prose-
cution brought out the wonderful courage and
constancy of this veritable hero, who was nearly
killed by torture, but recalled to life by the
devotion of his wife. Years afterwards, when
in Guyenne, Louis XIV. desired to see him, and
addressed him as 'Monsieur de Filhot, martyr
of my State.' He would never accept any
reward or the compensation Condé offered him
when, long after the events, he begged him to
forgive the wrong he had involuntarily done
him.

It was clear that everything that was best
in the country had finally turned against the
Fronde. It was dead in Paris and in all the
rest of the country. The turn of Bordeaux and
of the whole of Guyenne was very soon to
come. The Prince de Conti had definitely
concluded a treaty with the Court. There
only remained for him to get out of his present
awkward position and to escape from the tender
mercies of the Ormée in order to be as free
as he longed to feel. Madame la Princesse,

Anne-Geneviève, Marsin, and Lenet alone remained faithful to Condé and a lost cause. They made frantic efforts to secure the help of Spain at this juncture, and just for a moment there came a ray of hope, in the shape of formal proposals from Cromwell.[1] The feeble young Prince was tempted, even at the eleventh hour, to entertain them, and, if we are to believe. Cosnac, only prevented by him from actually doing so.

Mazarin, well informed of what was going on, now resolved to strike a great blow, and sent the Duc de Vendôme to besiege Bourg, which surrendered after three days.

So did Libourne and other cities. Bordeaux alone still held out. The Cardinal decided to leave it to itself, and again his plan succeeded perfectly. His only dread was the foreigner, so he sent Gourville to negotiate with Condé's representatives. Madame de Longueville and those who shared her responsibilities could not be won over: that he knew very well, but they were to be offered leave to withdraw from

[1] *Mémoires de Cosnac*, vol. i. p 68.

Bordeaux in safety, and it was better policy to do so than to seek revenge. Monsieur le Prince consented to an agreement by which he retained only his own troops, the officers to be free to leave him if they chose. The transaction was accepted by his wife, Madame de Longueville, Marsin, and Lenet, who, with the Prince de Conti, signed it on June 24, 1653. It was carried out within a few days. The Princess, with her son and Lenet, went to join her husband in Flanders. The Prince de Conti, accompanied by his little Court, retired to Languedoc, where he had a beautiful house, and led the life he might have been expected to lead. He was afterwards enriched at the expense of his elder brother, who was an exile, and by-and-by received the command of the army in Catalogne.[1] Madame de Longueville was absorbed by thoughts that were too deep for words, but had not had time to mature or shape themselves. She refrained from accom-

---

[1] Pouvoirs du Prince de Conty, Commandant Général en Catalogne, 4 mai, 1654, MS. 4188, fol. 261 (*Bibliothèque Nationale*).

panying her sister-in-law, and, having been given leave to withdraw to one of her houses, she started on her solitary journey to Montreuil-Bellay, one of her husband's places in Anjou. On August 3 the Dukes of Vendôme and Candale made their entry into Bordeaux. The red flag, then the symbol of the Ormée, as it has since been that of the Jacobins and of all extreme parties, had been removed from the church steeple of St. Michel, and the flag of France flew there once more as they drove to join in the ' Te Deum ' at St. André. The amnesty was loyally observed ; only one of the chiefs of the Ormée was executed after the barbarous fashion of the time. The town was restored to its normal condition as quickly as possible, and the endeavour of all was henceforth to forget a disastrous and inglorious civil war.

CHAPTER IV

THE PENANCE OF MADAME DE LONGUEVILLE.

PORT ROYAL

THE solitude of exile, disgrace, and poverty were now Madame de Longueville's portion in the present, and the future was uncertain. She did not know how long she would have to remain, virtually a prisoner, in her gloomy house, or what would be her husband's attitude towards her, and, having sacrificed all her personal property to her brother's cause, even to parting with her jewellery, she was for the moment utterly ruined. Far too proud before men to ask for any favours, the utmost to which she had been induced to consent was to let the Duc de Longueville use his endeavours at Court in the interest of their children, and she bravely and openly proclaimed her unvarying attachment to

Condé.   On October 25, 1653, she writes to
Lenet, then in the Netherlands with Monsieur
le Prince :

' The news from your quarters is the only
thing that really touches my heart, having no
real attachment but that which I have for my
brother.   I should be too happy if he were
persuaded of it, which I expect of his sense of
justice.   I think he has been informed of what
has been my conduct since my departure from
Bordeaux, and that he knows I have not sent to
the Court to ask for the amnesty.   Accordingly,
it has not granted it to me, in spite of all
Monsieur de Longueville has done.   He sends
me word that it is necessary, in his interest,
that I should write to the Court—that is, to the
King, to the Queen, and the Cardinal ; but as I
desire to do my duty to the end, and retain the
good fortune I have had of not being suspected,
even by my enemies, of having failed therein,
I have written to Monsieur de Longueville to
entreat him to approve of my not sending one
of my people to the Court, as I desire nothing
of them so long as my brother is in his present
condition ; that thus the thing concerned only
himself, and that it was but just he should
manage it alone ; that I would therefore send
him my letters, open, as they were necessary to
him, but that I implored him to let one of his
own people carry them, so that no face of any

one belonging to me should appear in a place
with which I could have no connection; but I
also begged him not to send my letter to the
Cardinal, unless it were absolutely necessary for
him.   That is all I have been able to contrive.
I send you the letters I have written, so that
you may judge whether the one to the Cardinal
could have been more moderate. . . .'

The first message she received from the
Court contained strict orders not to leave
Montreuil-Bellay before the Queen should have
come to a decision concerning her.   It was at
this moment of her deepest disgrace that
Madame de Longueville received for the second
time from the two brave Scudérys the most
courageous expression of sympathy that could
have been given to her.   When, on September 15, 1653, they published the tenth and last
volume of ' Le Grand Cyrus,' they again dedicated it to her who was, next to Condé, the
person most hated by the Queen and Mazarin.
The brother and sister could ill afford to be the
generous courtiers of misfortune they so persistently showed themselves, for, in addition to
their literary work, they had no other resources,

between them, than a small post to which
Georges de Scudéry had been appointed by the
Cardinal, and this the latter, who could be so
magnanimous when it was good policy to be so,
had the meanness to take from him in order to
punish him for his chivalrous friendship for
Madame de Longueville. She had literally
nothing left that was of any value except a
small portrait of herself framed in diamonds,
and this she sent to Monsieur and Mademoiselle
de Scudéry in token of her deep gratitude, a
feeling which never left her and which she
proved in every way when it was again to some
extent in her power to do so.[1]

After a little while she received the Queen's
permission to go to Moulins and stay at the
Convent of the Visitation with her aunt Marie
Félice des Ursins, Duchesse de Montmorency,
the widow of that brother of the dowager
Princess de Condé who had been executed at
Toulouse by order of Richelieu, an event which
had cast a gloom over Madame de Longueville's

[1] Lettre à Monsieur de Scudéry, ' de Louvré, le Vème avril.
MS. Fr. 12769, fol. 32–33 (*Bibliothèque Nationale*).

early childhood. Ever since that time his devoted widow had mourned and prayed for him in that religious house of which she had become the Superior, and where she led the life of a saint. She received her niece with the utmost affection, and, with a gentle hand and a profound insight into the needs of that complex but noble nature, she soothed and strengthened her and showed her the narrow way while she was yet groping in the darkness of uncertainty.

Every slander concerning Madame de Longueville was eagerly listened to at Court, and her enemies were as busy as ever trying to injure her. It was thus Madame de Montmorency, in religion Sister Marie Henriette, wrote the following letter to Monsieur de Longueville : [1]

'Moulins (Convent of the Visitation), April 2, 1654.

'I have heard from Madame la Duchesse de Longueville that, notwithstanding her wise and prudent conduct, she is taxed with having

[1] *Histoire des Princes de Condé.*

intrigues and receiving visits. . . . As for visits
she should not receive, she has received none,
nor even others. . . . I feel I must say what I
know. I should also wish to be able to tell of
the good actions of Her Highness and how much
I admire them ; but there are things which
words must diminish. . . . If one were to say
that she follows almost all the exercises of
religion, one would speak more truthfully, and
thereby one could prove that very little time is
left her for the parlour, where she only makes up
her mind to go with difficulty. . . . No person
of importance has been here, who has visited
her, so that I do not know on what this talk
can be based. . . . I assure you of her goodwill as of my own. If she had other thoughts,
she would not have chosen this place, or me for
her witness. . . . I should wish to have words.
strong enough, as her conduct is pure, to show
it to you in its brightness, and to represent to
you the reasonable and Christian feelings with
which she is filled. Those who honour her
cannot say all the good there is to be said. . . .
But I thought that those who are bestirring
themselves to forward her affairs will be glad to
have my evidence, which is according to the
unvarnished truth. . . . '

A few days before the date of this letter
Madame de Longueville wrote to the Comtesse
de Fiesque, the wife of Condé's confidential

agent in the Netherlands, whither both her husband and she had accompanied him, in a
manner which in the midst of all her anxiety
shows traces of the old sprightliness : [1]

' *To Madame la Comtesse de Fiesques.*

'From Moulins, March 28.

' The canvas is coarse and the piece is badly
conceived.   I praise God for it with all my
heart, for, after all, besides the interest of
Mademoiselle there is my own, and you see that
the beauty [*Madame de Châtillon*] who is in
question felt inclined to kill, as the common
saying is, two birds with one stone.   For, after
all, if Mademoiselle had written in that way,
one would have taken the mail, and no one
could doubt that I should have had a part in
the missive.   Well, we have there a good
friend who watches over us when we are asleep,
and who thinks of our interests when we neglect
them.   Truly this is the worthiest story that
lady has as yet invented, and I think you very
fortunate in having her in your neighbourhood,
so as to be amused from time to time by her
little plays.   I know a few of them, and I wish
he who is their principal subject [*Monsieur le*

[1] Victor Cousin's *Fragments Littéraires.* (Papiers de la
Maison de Grammont.)

Prince] were informed of it, because with all
those worries she spoils his affairs, for I know
there is nothing foolish she does not say in
order to show that she is his mistress.   It will
be a worthy action to do her a good turn in his
mind.   But he ought to break with her without
explanations.   I am going to pray, so as to
support thereby what you are going to do.   I
will be your saint in this enterprise, and it shall
be I who will ask God's blessing upon your
speech.   I should be delighted to write, but I
dare not, for if the mail were stopped Monsieur
de Longueville would never forgive me.   But
give a thousand messages for me [*to Condé*],
although without calling me by name, unless it be
that of his Martyr, for after all I am, the Prince
de Conty having said to Monsieur le Cardinal
that, if they let me return to Normandy, I
should place myself at the head of the disturbances my brother would cause there.   In fact,
Monsieur de Chenaille knows my affairs like
myself; and as the good man is not my confidant I can see that he has his information from
a lady who shares the secrets of the Minister
through her new admirer—I mean our assassin.
Truly, I am astonished at all this roguery ; that
is the real name for such a proceeding.   You
can write to me by way of the post, and put on
the outside of your letter ' To Monsieur Genin
at Moulins,' and inside, ' To Madame de Longueville.'   But we must have a cipher ; I am

asking for one.   You will use it so that we may
talk more freely, and above all of the poor absent
ones ; it is my only joy to have some news of
them and to suffer for them, at least, since I cannot serve them.   Pay my court to them, but in
all letters mention me only in cipher if you have
one.   But if the bearer of the letters is such as
you say, you may speak to him of me and my
new feelings, that he may speak about them only
to him who gives rise to them.   I have very
tender ones towards you, do not doubt it.   Let
me know how one can write to you.'

Madame de Longueville remained at Moulins
nearly eleven months, during which time the
example and influence of her admirable aunt
sank deeper and deeper into her heart.   Her
husband, who was now *persona grata* at Court,
the Princess Palatine, and Madame de Sablé
were all exerting themselves on her behalf.
At last they were successful,[1] and Monsieur de
Longueville was able to join his wife.   By-
and-by she had learned to conquer her pride,
and, as a first step in the career of renunciation

---

[1] Déclaration de Louis XIV en faveur de Madame la
Duchesse de Longueville, ' Chalons, au mois d'octobre 1653,'
Bibliothèque Nationale, MS. 4187, fol. 292.

and reparation on which she had resolved, she bowed her head before her husband. He was no hero, but a perfect gentleman, and he made it as easy for her as was in his power. On December 3, 1554, she wrote to Lenet from Acquigny :

' I am too much obliged to you for interesting yourself as you do in what concerns me. I do not doubt it, and on that basis I have been easily persuaded that you would be glad of my return to Monsieur de Longueville, who received me with infinite joy. He is here at present, and I have so little time to myself that I cannot write to you fully the particulars of my return, all of which are agreeable and such as I may be proud of, as I owe them solely to Monsieur de Longueville, and to the very end all my enemies have invariably opposed me. The Court has shown me great consideration at this juncture, and I have every reason to be satisfied as far as my personal interests are concerned. I ask nothing of God, now, but peace, and I ask of you the continuation of your friendship and that you may not doubt my own. My compliments to Monsieur de Marsin.'

A letter from the King written a few days later further improved her position.

To Madame la Duchesse de Longueville.[1]

'December 19, 1654.

' My Cousin—Now that I have the satisfaction I had promised myself of your conduct in permitting you to go to Louvières or to the house at Acquigny belonging to the de la Croisettes, I am willing to write you this letter, in order to tell you that I approve of your going to my town of Rouen, and wherever else you may wish to go within my province of Normandy ; and the present being written for no other purpose, I will make it longer only to pray God that He may have you, my cousin, in His holy and worthy keeping.'

Madame de Longueville's reconciliation to her husband was the symbol of the great change in her life. However, it was only the beginning, for she had now realised how much there was to be undone. Wherever possible, restitution must be made, and, where it was too late, she would at least atone by penance for the harm of which she had been the cause. Having once recognised the truth, she set herself to do her

---

[1] *Bibliothèque Nationale*, MS. Fr. 4189, föl. 295. Contemporary copy from the copybook of Monsieur Le Tellier (unpublished).

O

duty loyally, steadfastly, and indeed heroically. From the age of thirty-four, when she was still in the fulness of her beauty, her intellectual and personal charm, and her power of influencing others, she gave up every pleasure, every ambition, every thought of self, and devoted the rest of her life, without a single relapse, to home duties, good works, and to that austere penance which, in those days and with such a nature, was inseparable from a real 'conversion' such as hers.   Of this great mystic event in her life Madame de Longueville herself gave an account, which forms part of the general self-examination written down by her, years afterwards, by direction of her confessor.   One day, after reading a passage from some devotional book :

'It seemed to me,' she says, 'as if a curtain were drawn from before the eyes of my mind : all the charms of truth, united with a single object, presented themselves to me.   Faith, which had appeared, as it were, dead and buried under my passions, renewed itself.   I found myself like unto a person who, after a long sleep, where she had thought herself great, happy, honoured and esteemed by all, suddenly awakes and discovers herself to be in chains, wounded, downcast with languor, and shut up in a dungeon.'

During the twenty-five remaining years of her life she never failed to keep the anniversary of the day when, in this way, the truth had been revealed to her mind's eye.

For some years after this her own life, for the first time, has in it comparatively few landmarks. She spent the greater part of the year in Normandy, with her husband, looking after his health, which had begun to require a good deal of care, attending to his affairs and the duties he was no longer able to discharge, and devoting herself to the education of the two boys who were her only surviving children. Her constant preoccupation was to make up to her dependents and the population of the province in general for what they had suffered through her and her party, in their persons and property, and with this object she impoverished herself to the utmost. At first, in a spirit of self-humiliation, she allowed her religious life to be governed by an old parish priest, whose narrow views did not enable him to understand such a penitent, much less to guide her in accordance with her individual needs. Madame de Longueville resigned herself for many years to the round of mechanical religious exercises which, along with excessive austerities quite unsuited to her case, were all he could suggest for her edification. Monsieur de Longueville was much alarmed at the effect on her health of these practices, and later on, when at last she had a wiser director, he caused the latter to be informed of the extent to which they were being carried, in the hope that they might be kept within bounds. His love for his wife had quite returned, and he was full of admiration for her perseverance in the new life she was leading. His daughter's somewhat late marriage to the Duc de Nemours, by removing the disturbing influence of her undisguised ill-will towards her stepmother, helped to facilitate the life of Monsieur and Madame de Longueville. Now and again, though very rarely, she went to Paris to visit her beloved Carmelites, to whom more than ever she longed to be entirely united, and her old friend, Madame de Sablé, as well as her new sister-in-law. On February 22, 1654, the Prince de Conti had been married to the good and beautiful Anne Martinozzi, the best of Mazarin's nieces, who became, and remained throughout her short life, a real friend to Madame de Longueville.

On March 27 of the same year Condé, who was still engaged in a treacherous war against his country in the Netherlands, had been in his absence solemnly condemned to death and deprived of all his possessions. Fortunately for his House, the sentence of confiscation did not affect his posterity, for nothing was to be touched for five years, and by the time that period had elapsed the Peace of the Pyrenees was about to be signed, and Condé was allowed to return to France. It may be imagined how the heart of his ever-devoted sister went out to him ; and the following letter, although of a somewhat later date, shows to what extent her thoughts were always with the exile : [1]

[1] *Histoire des Princes de Condé*, vol. vi.

The Duchesse de Longueville to Monsieur
le Prince.

'Trie, November 14, 1657.

'On my return from Caen I heard of your illness, and although I am assured on your behalf that it is nothing dangerous, I cannot obey your command not to trouble myself about it, for I confess I do so to an extent which cannot be imagined. It is at such times one feels with redoubled violence the grief one always feels at your unfortunate absence, and one cannot console oneself for not being able to run after you, both in order to see you and to serve you. In God's name, have the charity to give orders that news of you may be sent me regularly as long as your illness lasts, for I can bear it no longer. We have just arrived from Caen, where I wanted to have my children painted for you; but there are such wretched artists there that I prefer to do nothing of the kind, rather than let you see their faces as if they were worse-looking than they are, having too much the interest and the wish that they should please you. The first time we go to see them I will take an artist from Paris, in order to send them to you. But this is not the moment to tire you with a long letter. I must finish it, and assure you that if my prayers were good you would soon be perfectly cured and entirely satisfied.

'Farewell, my dear brother. I am altogether yours.'

In 1655 we hear of Madame de Longueville
at Bourbon-les-Bains, whither she had accompanied her husband, who was to take the
waters there. The numerous friends she met
on that occasion tell of her kindness to all, and
of her princely benefactions. Among others,
she provided for large numbers of poor
patients in need of the waters, and who could
not otherwise have enjoyed their good effects.
A letter from the clever pen of the Comtesse
de Maure,[1] the intimate friend of Madame de
Sablé, who had been, as well as her husband,
a prominent member of the Fronde, gives an
amusing account of the ridiculous scenes caused
by the airs the Duchesse de Bouillon gave
herself in the little watering-place. The Duke
and Duchess had joined the Fronde mainly
in order to recover their principality of Sedan,
incorporated with the Crown in 1643. For
this they had eventually obtained compensation
in the shape of money and another purely
honorary principality. The Duchess was therefore entitled, strictly speaking, to the rank of a

[1] Victor Cousin, *Madame de Sablé.*

princess, but certainly not to being called Her Highness, and in this she would by no means acquiesce. Madame de Longueville tried to throw oil on the troubled waters, but even her tact and skill were unsuccessful. Another letter was written by Mademoiselle de Vandy, Madame de Maure's niece, to the Duchesse de Longueville after she had left Bourbon. It is interesting in so far as it shows that the beauty and charm of her correspondent were still as great as ever:

'. . . If your Highness were only a Bourbon, if you had not a complexion like a pearl, the mind and gentleness of an angel, the Highnesses you have left behind you would not be able to comfort us for your absence. . . .'

The friendship of the Princess Palatine and that of Madame de Sablé were among the great features of Madame de Longueville's life at this period, and the intercourse with them afforded her the only social and intellectual pleasure in which she had not ceased to indulge. To these names must be added that of Mademoiselle de Vertus, the admirable sister

of the notorious Duchesse de Montbazon, who
became Madame de Longueville's constant
and most helpful companion, and remained so
until she retired to Port Royal. These four
friends are most characteristic types of that
ardent religious fervour of which the great
ladies of that time, so often accused of frivolity,
were capable when once they had been
'touched by grace.' The story of the 'conversion' of the Princess Palatine, who had been
a freethinker, and whose private life had been
by no means blameless, is told by Bossuet
in language of unsurpassed magnificence.[1]
Mademoiselle de Vertus knew and despised
the world and its pleasures, from which she
had withdrawn without having to reproach herself with any grave fault, in order to give
herself up to ardent piety and good works.
Madeleine de Souvré, Marquise de Sablé,
was quite different from each of the others.
In her youth she had been one of the greatest
ornaments of the Hôtel de Rambouillet, and
the early love of that Duc de Montmorency

[1] Bossuet, *Oraison Funèbre de la Princesse Palatine.*

to whose tragic end reference has been made. Her marriage to the Marquis was no very happy one; but she was always extremely popular and respected, literary in her tastes, and religious in a quiet moderate way, which did not exclude the pleasures of life. At her husband's death in 1640 she lost a considerable part of her money, and two years later the great grief of her life overtook her through the death in battle of her favourite son, Guy de Laval. She then left the Quartier du Louvre, and lived for some time in the Place Royale, where her *salon* became celebrated. A few years later she exchanged her house there for Port Royal, where she was able to enjoy the religious support and sympathy of the excellent nuns, and at the same time continue to receive her friends without interfering with the life of the community. Part of the buildings of Port Royal de Paris are still in existence; among others, the pretty brown brick house with its seventeenth-century gables which Madame de Sablé built for herself in the outer courtyard of the celebrated monastery. It is situated in what was then the Rue de la Bourbe, and has now been turned into the broad and commonplace Boulevard de Port Royal, not far from the Carmelites of the Faubourg St. Jacques. During the Revolution it was used as a prison, and is now the Maternity Hospital of Paris. Of the beautiful church only the severely simple choir is left, nearly opposite to Madame de Sablé's house. Some of the wards show the divisions of the cells, and a portion of the original gardens is left. Such as it is, Port Royal is still worth a visit from those who take any interest in the inner life of the men and women of the seventeenth century in France.

The little gabled house within its precincts became the home of that new literary *genre* which is associated with Madame de Sablé almost as closely as it is with La Rochefoucauld. The 'Maxims' and 'Portraits,' which soon became 'the rage' with all the polished society of that period, and which he brought to a point of perfection, were practically invented by her, and thus she had the honour of being to a certain extent the literary parent of Pascal's

'Pensées' and the 'Caractères de La Bruyère.' As almost every one of those whose privilege it was to be intimate with the Marquise wrote 'Portraits,' Mademoiselle imitated and developed the fashion at her little Court in the Luxembourg, and, before that fastidious literary artist, La Rochefoucauld, felt satisfied that his perfectly chiselled, cynical sayings were really fit to be published, they had been carefully submitted to Madame de Sablé and all those members of her charmed circle who were best fitted to judge and criticise them. The Marquise, whom in her youth Victor Cousin describes as 'the perfect Précieuse,' was good-nature in person. She was an excellent hostess, the favourite and ever-kindly intermediary in all manner of difficulties, and often a wise counsellor. There is good reason for supposing that it was she who, as early as the time when Madame de Longueville was at Stenay, suggested the marriage of the Prince de Conti with Mazarin's niece as a way out of all existing difficulties. She was a good and faithful friend, with little weaknesses which amused her acquaintances and often irritated Mother Agnès Arnauld when Superior of Port Royal. One of these small shortcomings was her terror of illnesses, malaria, and everything that could affect her health. In one of the rare little notes that have been preserved of Madame (Henrietta of England), with whom she was a great favourite, the Princess·tells her, *à propos* of this well-known foible, that she is afraid to keep her appointment to come and see Madame de Sablé because she has a cold, of which the sight alone might make her correspondent sick. Another weakness was the importance she attached to the dainties of the table, which, after she had come to live at Port Royal, contrasted strangely with her austere surroundings. Her letters are, therefore, often an amusing mixture of intellectual questions and religious topics, interspersed with recipes for a new dish and prescriptions against every disease on the face of the earth. Even when writing to her Carmelite friends, especially Marthe du Vigean, she mentions the jellies she is sending across to their convent, and which

the nuns give to their invalids.   Yet she had
her serious side.   She was the authoress of two
essays, one on Friendship, and one on Education, which is a valuable contribution.   Largely
under the influence of the admiration she felt
for the noble sacrifice Madame de Longueville
had made of all that was precious to her, she
also was 'converted.'   As Victor Cousin
defines it,

'the religious feelings she shared with her
contemporaries assumed a more pronounced
character;' but, he adds, 'in thinking more
about God she did not change her nature,
and remained herself.   With her turn of mind,
her taste for the distinction and importance to
which she was accustomed, she could not be
satisfied with ordinary piety; after having been
a *Précieuse*, she became refined in her devout-
ness.   Always aiming at the sublime, like the
women of her youth, she exchanged the
Spanish *galanterie* for Jansenism.'[1]

To this motive may be added the long-
standing intimacy with such eminent adepts
of the doctrine of Jansenius as Madame de
Guyméné, Monsieur d'Andilly, brother of the

---

[1] *Madame de Sablé.*

great Arnauld, and *la grande Mère Angélique*. It was for all these reasons that, when it became necessary for Madame de Sablé to find quarters at once suited to her rank and her reduced fortune, half in the world and yet half out of it, she sought and found an ideal harbour of refuge in the little dwelling, leaning for support against the monastery, which she built for herself in 1655.

As it was to the Marquise de Sablé that Port Royal and the cause of the Jansenists owed Madame de Longueville, the origin of the former's attachment to that party is of interest for those who study the life of her most intimate friend.

In 1662, when Madame de Longueville was living in complete retirement, there fell upon her the blow which, after years of repentance on her part, and of gradual forgetfulness on that of others, brought back to public notice the story of her past errors, exaggerated and disfigured by one man's cowardly malice. The ' Mémoires sur le Règne de la Reine Anne ' appeared in the course of that year, and were feebly disavowed by their real author, the Duc de La Rochefoucauld, whose act of deferred revenge was one of the most cruel ever committed. The following letter, which was afterwards appended to the edition published by Belin, was, there is every reason to suppose, addressed to Madame de Sablé :

‘ Two-thirds of the book shown to me, which is said to be current under my name, are not by me, and I have no part therein. The other third, which is near the end, is so altered and falsified in all its parts, and in the sense, the order, and the terms, that there is hardly anything in conformity with what I had written on that subject. That is why I disavow it as a thing assumed by my enemies, or by the dishonesty of those who sell all manner of manuscripts under whatever name they choose to put. Madame de Sablé, Monsieur de Liancourt, and Monsieur Esprit have seen what I have written for myself alone. They know it is quite different from that which has been set in circulation, and that there is nothing therein which is not as it should be, in so far as it concerns Monsieur le Prince. . . . The same thing must be said of what concerns Madame de Longueville.’

Again, when he became aware that his

victim and her brother had expressed their indignation at the way in which he had treated her, it was to Madame de Sablé he wrote to complain of their complaints :

'They give me such different accounts of her feelings towards me,' he says, 'that I confess you would oblige me extremely by telling me candidly what you have observed, for, to speak frankly, I cannot understand how a person who every day gives proofs of such extraordinary piety could have preferred to complain of me with bitterness, and accuse me of having composed a work which she well knows I have not written, rather than believe in the explanations you have given her. . . .'

Madame de Longueville was spared no humiliation. Her friends, it is true, were very angry, and drew closer round her, but those libellous stories made their way among all classes of society, even those who had known nothing about them before.

The one great and consoling event of this portion of her life was the submission, in 1659, of her brother, who, after the signature of the

P

Peace of the Pyrenees,[1] returned to France. The clauses in the Treaty relating to him had been the cause of some delay, as Mazarin continued to dread the influence of Condé, and still more so that of his sister, although she had so nearly cut herself off from the world. On the other hand, Don Luis de Haro, the Spanish Plenipotentiary, would not listen to any arrangement which excluded from its operation the man to whom Spain owed so much. When at last every resistance had been overcome, and peace was an accomplished fact, Monsieur le Prince was well received and frankly taken into favour again by the Court. Madame de Longueville, with her husband and her two sons, met him at Coulomniers [2] on his arrival from Brussels, and at the former place Madame la Princesse, coming from Flanders joined them within a few days.

[1] 'Acceptation faicte par Monsieur le Prince de Condé du traicté de paix des Pyrenées en ce qui le regarde. Faict à Bruxelles le 26 novembre 1669' (*Bibliothèque Nationale*, MS. 4240, fol. 132).

[2] Erection de Coulomniers en duché-pairie en faveur du Duc de Longueville, Paris, May 1654 (*Bibliothèque Nationale*, 4188, fol. 256).

When the brother and sister met they felt that, whatever changes there might be in both, their love for each other was unaltered and the past forgotten. Owing to the recent death of Gaston, Duc d'Orléans, he was now, next to the King's brother, his nearest relation. The fact that he served his country faithfully and successfully ever after, and in due course was himself 'converted,' and did all in his power to make up for what others had suffered through his instrumentality, was to Madame de Longueville a lasting consolation.

It was about this time that the active persecutions against the Jansenists began which were, for so long, to disturb the peace of the Church and the consciences of right-minded and tolerant people. Towards the end of the year 1660 Madame de Longueville had failed to visit the Marquise de Sablé on one of the rare occasions when she came to Paris for a short time. In answer to her old friend's re-proaches, insinuating that she had been afraid to come and see a Jansenist, she writes on December 31 :

'All the Jansenism in the world would not have prevented me from coming to see you, had I been longer or more at liberty in Paris.'

Early in the New Year she says :

' The noise carried on around you will not prevent my visiting you.   Had it not already been my intention, I should immediately resolve to do so now.   I shall see you, then, on Wednesday, and we will talk about this affair.'

After having talked about it, she desired to become acquainted with *la grande Mère Angélique*, for whom Madame de Sablé felt the veneration that was shared by all who knew her.

' Alas !' writes Madame de Longueville, ' how I feel all you tell me and not being able to relieve the necessity to which these poor creatures have been reduced !   I wish as ardently I had some money, in order to give it to them, as a miser wishes for it in order to shut it up in a chest.'

It was a fact that, at this time, Madame de Longueville was reduced almost to penury by the generosity which had prompted her, as well as her sister-in-law the Princesse de Conti,

to involve themselves in endless acts of restitution, and, during a famine, to feed, between
them, almost the entire population of districts
which had been ruined by the Fronde.

Great was the impression produced on the
Duchess by her interview with the venerable
Abbess of Port Royal, who was dying like the
saint she had been all her life. She was racked
with anxiety for the future of her beloved
monastery. Yet, ever desirous of avoiding
anything theatrical or opposed to the most
exalted spirit of monastic humility, she hardly
dared to speak to the Sisters lest they should
write down every word she uttered for purposes
of controversy. Mother Angélique Arnauld
fell under the spell of the heroine of the
Fronde, whom she had expected to find so
different. She was charmed with her gentleness and simplicity.

'All I have seen of that Princess,' she wrote
to Madame de Sablé, 'has seemed to me of the
finest gold.'

In August 1661, Mother Angélique expired,
and her eyes were no sooner closed than the

storm she had dreaded broke over her house, and her nuns were dispersed in all directions.

Madame de Sablé would not take advantage of her name, which, doubtless, would have secured immunity for herself, but took refuge with her friends, chiefly at the Hôtel de Longueville, which also became, eventually, the haven of rest for the persecuted leaders of the party. Madame de Longueville and her House had only just made their peace with the Court and those in power. But all the brave chivalry of her nature was stirred up, and, at the risk of whatever might be the consequences to herself, she openly declared for Port Royal and Jansenism, whose cause she never abandoned till she had brought about, single-handed, that great achievement of her life described as 'the Peace of the Church.'

Her courageous devotion had its reward in the immense blessing which came to her when she secured as her director that severe but admirable spiritual guide, Monsieur Singlin, the confessor of Port Royal. He was of humble origin, the son of a wine merchant, who had been apprenticed to a draper until the age of twenty-two, when some sudden impulse brought him to 'Monsieur Vincent' (St. Vincent de Paul), who advised him to become a priest, although he did not even know a word of Latin. The saintly head of the 'Prêtres des Missions' helped him through his studies and secured for him an appointment as chaplain to a hospital, where he was introduced to the great Abbé de St. Cyran, then already director of Port Royal. He begged to be allowed to become one of his disciples, and Monsieur de St. Cyran soon recognised in this particularly humble penitent the special qualifications which he demanded of a confessor. He compelled Monsieur Singlin, much against his will, to exercise all the functions of the priesthood, of which the latter believed himself unworthy, particularly those of preacher and confessor. He became the director, not only of Madame de Longueville, but of many of the greatest personages of the time, and one of his most marked characteristics was the dignity and authority which never for a moment left him, once he had been induced to undertake the spiritual guidance of their lives. This, in her case, was throughout wise and moderate. He constantly dwelt on the paramount importance of making reparation, of subduing that pride and vanity which had been at the root of all her mistakes and wrong-doings ; and, as long as he lived, he restrained to some extent her exaggerated tendency to self-mortification. It was Mademoiselle de Vertus, now her almost inseparable companion, who prevailed on Monsieur Singlin to under-take the case of her friend at a time when she was particularly troubled in her mind. The state of affairs in regard to the Jansenists was such that the first visits he paid to Madame de Longueville involved a considerable risk to himself, and he had to go to her house, with the long wig of the period, disguised as a physician.

In May 1663, Monsieur de Longueville died, and after that the Duchess resided more constantly in Paris, either at her own house or at the Carmelites, where she had a lodging within the precincts. This enabled her to take up the cause of the persecuted in a still more effectual manner, and to that task she mainly devoted the years that immediately followed.

The seventeenth century is the period of the deepest religious earnestness and the most absorbing spiritual life in France, and the fact is the more striking from the juxtaposition of that which immediately precedes and that which immediately follows it. Springing from the artistic paganism of the sixteenth century, and resulting in the mocking and contemptuous freethought of the eighteenth, it would almost seem as if the former led up directly to the latter, and the great intervening epoch had nothing to do with their natural course of development. The superhuman renouncement and asceticism of the Abbé de Rancé, the founder of the Trappists, the sweet reasonableness of the direction of souls of St. Francis de Sales, the ardent practical charity of St. Vincent de Paul, and the exalted virtues, intellectual superiority, and admirable human service, coupled with indomitable energy and spiritual pride, of Port Royal and its numerous followers, all existed at the same time. Each of these names represents only one of the most characteristic schools of thought and centres of action, and each meant reform in some direction.

Port Royal was associated with a spiritual revolution, and its members became the martyrs of a needlessly cruel repression. To that and to the fact that it was the nucleus round which collected men and women endowed with the greatest minds and the strongest characters is due its paramount importance. Port Royal was a great organism which grew and developed according to the laws of its own being, not the work of one founder or even of the remarkable family to whom it owed its existence. We are too apt to identify Jansenism and Port Royal, but they are not one and the same thing. The great Abbey and its surrounding ' Thébaïde ' of learned hermits would have been possible without Jansenius. But, given the doctrine of the Bishop of Ypres, it was inevitable that the leading minds of Port Royal should gravitate towards it ; and, given the stuff these heroes and heroines of religious life were made of, it was clear that, once adopted, they would stand or fall by views which we should find it hard to defend on their own merits.

Their original house stood in the deep and somewhat gloomy valley of Chevreuse, a good deal of which was then a swamp, not very many miles from Versailles, in what is now the department of Seine-et-Oise. In those days, when the grand and sombre aspects of Nature had not begun to appeal to people's tastes, the spot struck them as 'a horrible desert,' and this notion gave rise to the name of ' *le désert* ' constantly referred to when ' *ces Messieurs de Port Royal* ' or ' *les Solitaires,*' as they were alternately called, took up their abode in the outer precincts of the ancient monastery. Its origin and that of the name it bore are wrapt in darkness and legend, but it was certainly founded in 1204 by Mathilde de Garland as an ex-voto for the safe return of her husband, Mathieu I. de Montmorency-Marli, from the fourth crusade, and the most ancient charters call it ' Porros.' It was first under the Cistercian rule, then under that of St. Bernard, and, until

the end of the sixteenth century it went through
the usual stages of indifference and decay.   In
1599 happened the small event which was to
change its fate and give it a place in history.
The last insignificant Abbess was induced to
take for a 'coadjutress' the little girl of seven
who became the great Mother Angélique, the
reformer of her monastery, through whom, by-
and-by, almost all the members of the Arnauld
family were brought into more or less direct
connection with Port Royal.   The child disliked
the religious life.   Nevertheless, by the time
she had attained the age of sixteen she had
determined to carry out the great reform,
obtained the consent of her reluctant nuns,
overcome every obstacle, and persuaded her
father and mother, whom she devotedly loved,
to accept the new claustration, which forbade
them access to the convent.

The father and grandfather of the two
generations of remarkable men and women
who made Port Royal what it became was
a brilliant advocate much appreciated by
Henri IV.   Many of his great speeches have

been preserved, and in 1594 he pleaded for the University of Paris against the Jesuits. The two great Mothers, Angélique and Agnès, 'the great Arnauld,' Monsieur d'Andilly, and five nuns, all more or less distinguished, were his children. Mother Angélique de St. Jean, Messieurs le Maître, de Sacy, and de Séricourt were his grandchildren. Madame Arnauld joined the community after she had become a widow.

On All Saints' Day, 1608, the Abbess was 'touched by Grace,' and began her reformation. She turned her house into a kind of Paradise of saints. One day, at her bidding, her nuns received thirty penniless Sisters, who had become homeless, into their convent which was barely large enough for themselves, and with these they joyfully shared their last crust. For many years, during her early difficulties, she was guided by that most lovable of directors, St. Francis de Sales, Bishop of Geneva, whose friend and confidant she was almost to the same extent as Madame de Chantal, the foundress of the Order of the Visitation, and the future saint. It was, however, after his death, when a very different spiritual pastor had succeeded him, that the monastery developed into that unique institution which the name of Port Royal calls up in our minds. This was the Abbé de St. Cyran, Jean du Vergier de Hauranne. He was born at Bayonne in 1581, and distinguished himself by the most thorough theological studies, which he continued at Louvain. There he met Jansenius, and the close friendship formed by these two men was the origin of the great theological controversy with which Port Royal will always be identified. He received the Abbey of St. Cyran in 1620, and about the end of that year became acquainted with M. d'Andilly, still at that time a very successful man of the world, who almost at once induced his new friend and his sister, Mother Angélique, to enter into a correspondence. It was also about this time that the new theories concerning the meaning and teaching of St. Augustine, which became the doctrine of Jansenius, began to crystallise. An interview took place between him and St. Cyran.

The one was a voluminous writer and more like a mediæval scholar, the other a practical, uncompromising theologian and reformer. It is pretty certain that, then and there, they came to an understanding as to the resurrection of the doctrine of 'Grace,' which was to become the centre and pivot of a warfare, disastrous in itself, but which brought out and tempered the character of a large number of truly admirable women and men. In 1634, at a difficult moment in the government of her house, Mother Angélique accepted St. Cyran as confessor to Port Royal. A few years later he made M. Singlin his second, and the latter became the confessor, whereas the Abbé remained the director of the convent. It was no longer the old house to which Mothers Angélique and Agnès were so deeply attached. In 1625 the community had removed to what was henceforth known as Port Royal de Paris, to distinguish it from Port Royal des Champs. The latter had become much too small for the number of inmates, and increasingly unhealthy. It was not till the year 1638 that there began to be

formed, under St. Cyran's direction and inspired
by him, that wonderful little group of 'hermits,'
mostly laymen, who went to live in the outer
precincts of Port Royal des Champs, then
deserted by the nuns. It was in no sense an
order, or even a society, and to each were
assigned his special functions. The objects of
their lives were 'penance,' study, and the education of a few boys, among whom was to be
Racine. Such was the origin of the excellent
schools, corresponding to those for girls created
by the nuns, which *ces Messieurs* carried on as
long as they were allowed to do so, and for
which was written the celebrated 'Logic.' In
the organisation of this growing institution,
as well as in his guidance of the convent,
St. Cyran always showed himself what Sainte-
Beuve, in his fascinating history of Port
Royal,[1] has defined so well as 'the Christian
director *par excellence*, rigorous, truthful, rigid,
and a safe physician of the soul.' But to the
outside world he was absolutely uncompromising. Sources of irritation against the

[1] C. A. Sainte-Beuve, *Port Royal.*

Jansenists had, moreover, been accumulating for a long time. A pamphlet called 'Mars Gallicus,' published by Jansenius in 1635, in which he attacked the prerogatives of the King of France and the policy of Richelieu, had created much annoyance, and was remembered by the latter when the opportunity presented itself of being avenged on the Jansenists. St. Cyran's theological works, mainly his 'Petrus Aurelius,' and his subsequent refusal of a bishopric, led up to the first great blow to Port Royal—the imprisonment in 1638 of the Abbé in the dungeon of Vincennes, where he remained to within a short time of his death. The 'hermits' were dispersed. 'Had Luther and Calvin been shut up before they began to dogmatise,' said Richelieu on that occasion, ' the States would have been spared many disturbances.'

A week before the arrest of Monsieur de St. Cyran, Jansenius died, leaving the manuscript of the famous 'Augustinus,' to which his friend had doubtless contributed to a consider-

Q

able extent, ready for publication. It did not, however, leave the printing press of Louvain till the year 1640, after many unavailing efforts on the part of the Jesuits to prevent its appearance. Several editions followed in France, and fierce rejoinders were forthcoming. In 1643, when, at last, St. Cyran was set at liberty—he died the same year— he caused the great Arnauld to write in its defence. In fact, the war of the pen never stopped, and since the Middle Ages no Latin work on theology had created such an uproar. This too celebrated book was, in reality, nothing but a complete arrangement, in a particular order, and with a view to proving a particular doctrine, of all that St. Augustine has written on the subject of the degeneracy of human nature, and the exclusive saving power of Grace, accompanied by historical and psychological comments thereon by Jansenius himself. The corollaries of the two fundamental statements are, of course, predestination and the complete loss of man's freedom of choice since the original sin. The stand taken by the author is practically the infallibility of St. Augustine.

The first of the famous 'Five Propositions,' supposed to be contained in the book, which were eventually condemned by the Roman Curia, is the following :

'Aliqua Dei præcepta hominibus justis volentibus et conantibus, secundum præsentes quas habent vires sunt impossibilia, deest quoque iis gratia qua possibilia fiant.'

('Some of God's precepts are impossible to the just, however strong their will and their endeavour, according to their present strength, and the grace by which they would be possible is absent.')

This proposition differs from the four others that were condemned, inasmuch as it is actually in the text of the book in so many words, whereas the others are 'implied' or 'inferred.'

The matter is no longer of sufficient interest to be gone into more fully. It was, however, on this work, and one other, the 'Moral Reflections' by Père Quesnel, that the persecutions of Port Royal were based. Mazarin cared but little about ecclesiastical controversies, and only yielded to pressure in regard to them, but Louis XIV. took up a strong line of his own, and acted accordingly, when he began to reign alone.

Madame de Motteville writes of the year 1647 :

'The talk in Paris was of nothing but the Jansenists and the Molinists. That question, in which there was no one who was not interested for the satisfaction of his conscience, divided not only the schools, but the *ruelles*, the town as well as the Court. Those who were called the Molinists, from Molina, the Spanish Doctor, had in their favour the censure of the five propositions of the book of Jansenius, and those who were called Jansenists maintained that the five propositions which had been condemned were not in the book. That defence, their entirely exemplary lives, and the severity which they professed, secured for them the esteem of many persons of solid piety. . . . The Queen (Anne of Austria) took, at once, the part of the Jesuits, who had the advantage of governing the conscience of the King. She believed it to be her duty to oppose opinions which were supposed to be new, and which might create disturbances in the Church.'

To this unlucky controversy, the terrible rigidity of St. Cyran and of the majority of *ces Messieurs*, and the heroic obstinacy of the nuns, sacrificed the useful and noble work of Port Royal. They preferred to die or suffer anything rather than admit, against their conscience, that something was in a book (the 'Augustinus') which the Sisters declared they had never read, in which they believed it was not. Jansenius and his doctrines are profoundly uninteresting to most of us. But it must not be forgotten that they caused Pascal to write his immortal 'Lettres Provinciales.' He also joined the 'hermits' after his 'conversion,' in consequence of his miraculous escape from a terrible accident, and through the instrumentality of his sister. Jacqueline Pascal, in religion Sœur St. Euphémie, was a woman of genius who, in obedience to her vocation, buried in the cloister poetical and other gifts of a high order. She died of a broken heart, because, by direction of her superiors, she had signed the 'Formulary' in spite of her own conscientious objections.

Corneille, as well as Racine, was deeply and lastingly influenced by Port Royal. Nicole wrote his ' Essais de Morale' under its influence. It revolutionised education, and the character of two generations was moulded largely by the new ideas on the subject which it introduced.

It is this intellectual superiority of the unique little world gathered round the great Abbey, and, still more, the moral greatness of those saintly nuns, which attract us to Port Royal, after more than two centuries; and it was that greatness which drew Madame de Longueville to the centre of Jansenism, far more than its doctrine and the dispute about free-will and Grace, which she adopted as part of the institution she admired and took under her protection. That she did adopt it, with characteristic whole-heartedness, and quite openly, is proved by a little anecdote told by Villefore. There had been a long discussion at the King's toilet between the Archbishop of Embrun, who believed a certain libellous pamphlet against himself to be the work of the

Jansenists, the Duc de Montausier, husband of Mademoiselle de Rambouillet, and the Prince de Condé, who chaffed the Prelate unmercifully for some time. Coming out of the King's room, Monsieur le Prince met the latter's brother, Maréchal de la Feuillade, who was as angry as the Archbishop, and began to talk of 'cutting off the noses of all the Jansenists.' 'Ah, Monsieur le Maréchal,' said the Prince, laughingly, 'I crave your mercy for the nose of my sister.' La Rochefoucauld, analysing her with his usual keenness, describes how amenable Madame de Longueville was to personal influence. She had conversed with 'la grande Mère Angélique,' and was well acquainted with Mother Agnès, whose portrait has been preserved in Philippe de Champagne's picture, now at the Louvre, recording the miraculous cure of his daughter in answer to her prayers. The Duchess also knew Mother Angélique de St. Jean, who suffered a cruel imprisonment in a strange convent in consequence of her refusal to sign the celebrated 'Formulary.' In the agony of the

solitude by means of which her persecutors
and gaolers endeavoured to reduce her to submission she went through the most tragic
conflict the human and religious mind can have
to face. She was compelled by her superiors
to write an account of these experiences, and,
in its terrible earnestness, without any literary
art, it is one of the most moving human documents one can read. Madame de Longueville,
whose own moral and physical courage had
never given way, must have felt irresistibly
drawn towards such characters as these. Port
Royal appealed to her love of action and
grandeur, as the Carmelites with their simple
saintliness and mystic idealism satisfied her heart
and her imagination.

The famous 'Formulaire' for which the
younger Mother Angélique had suffered so
much, for which Monsieur de Sacy spent two
years at the Bastille, and which killed Jacqueline
Pascal, whilst it broke the heart of many
obscurer martyrs, was decreed by the assembly
of the clergy after they had accepted the first
Papal Bull against Jansenius in 1655. It was

ordered to be signed by every priest and, sub-
sequently, by every nun.

Its wording was as follows :

'I submit myself sincerely to the constitution of our Holy Father Pope Innocent X. . . .
and I condemn, with my heart and mouth, the
doctrine of the Five Propositions of Cornelius
Jansenius contained in his book "Augustinus,"
which has been condemned by the Pope and
the Bishops, which doctrine is not that of St.
Augustine, which Jansenius has badly explained,
contrary to the true meaning of that holy
Doctor.'

The decree of his predecessor having been
confirmed by Alexander VII. in a new Bull, on
October 16, 1656, the submission to this second
Bull was afterwards added to the 'Formulary.'

But the Parliament of Paris could only be
induced to register either by the actual presence
of the King, who always took up a strong
personal attitude in the controversy. This
fact is sufficiently explained by a previous
quotation from Madame de Motteville's
Memoirs. Although the Queen-Mother died
in 1666, her influence with her son survived
her. Cardinal Mazarin, on the other hand,

with characteristic indifference to everything that did not belong to the domain of politics, was tired of the whole affair, which gave him more trouble than weightier matters. The carrying out of the decree therefore remained in abeyance until 1660. It was then the persecution became acute and general, and it reached its height after Mazarin's death, on March 9th, 1661, followed in August by that of the great Mother Angélique, the prestige of whose name had to some extent protected her monastery. Not long after those events, the nuns who had refused to sign were dispersed and sent into captivity, from which they were released only because the King preferred not to continue the payment of the pensions due to the various convents in which they were kept prisoners. They were then sent to their old Abbey of Port Royal des Champs, which was by now utterly unfit to receive them. Here they were kept, practically, in a state of siege, being barely allowed fresh air and exercise enough to keep them alive in an overcrowded house. The handiwork of the ' hermits ' had not succeeded in making the surroundings healthy, and the ranks of the Sisters were decimated by fever. Deprived of the one supreme consolation of the Sacrament of the Altar, they were comforted only, after a time, by the devoted charity of that admirable 'Solitaire,' Monsieur Hamon, who allowed himself to be made a prisoner with them in order to succour them, both as a physician and a priest.

The active intervention of Madame de Longueville on behalf of Port Royal really began in the year preceding the Cardinal's death. The dispersion of the Sisters had also made *ces Messieurs* homeless, and they were safe nowhere. She began by throwing all her houses open to them. The safety of Nicole, the author of the ' Essais de Morale,' so greatly appreciated by his contemporaries, and of Arnauld, whose book ' De la Fréquente Communion,' had created a storm, was threatened most, and their presence was most compromising at that time. They were received at the Hôtel de Longueville itself, as well as Dr. de Lalane, and there the Duchess hid them

successfully for many months. With regard to
the crucial question of the 'Formulary' she had
passed through different phases of opinion. At
first, like her guests, she was in favour of signing it as an act of obedience. Afterwards she
advocated qualified signature, under protest; and
finally, her true nature gaining the upper hand,
she declared for unqualified refusal, with all its
consequences of suffering, for the sake of conscience.

Four of the most courageous among the
Bishops had taken the part of Port Royal after
the second Bull in 1665. These were the
saintly M. Pavillon, Bishop of Aleth; Henri
Arnauld, Bishop of Angers, brother of the
learned doctor and of M. d'Andilly and
Mother Angélique; M. de Buzanval, Bishop
of Beauvais; and M. de Caulet, Bishop of
Pamiers, once a disciple of St. Vincent de Paul.
Among those who were ready to assist her in
the long and complicated negotiations she had
undertaken in the interest of pacification, the
foremost was M. de Gondrin, Archbishop of
Sens, who had the ear of the King. They also

included her old friend and correspondent
M. Godeau, Bishop of Vence, who, at first, had
consented himself to sign the 'Formulary,' and
the son of Madame de Sablé, M. de Laval,
Bishop of La Rochelle. At the suggestion of
M. de Gondrin, with whom she discussed every
step in this difficult campaign, and urged on
also by Mademoiselle de Vertus, she wrote a
letter to the new Pope, Clement IX., on July
27, 1667, accompanied by another to Cardinal
Azzolini, in which she laid before His Holiness
the case of the poor nuns, and, incidentally, that
of 'ces Messieurs de Port-Royal' and the four
Bishops.

'What I can say truthfully,' she wrote to the
supreme Pontiff, 'concerning the Jansenists, is
that theirs is the greatest and the smallest party
in the world, at once the strongest and the
weakest . . . consisting as it does of a dozen
pious and clever theologians who have been
persecuted for twenty years, and whose pretended errors can be reduced to a question of
fact, on which they only defend themselves
because occasion is taken to treat them as
heretics. . . . They have always been very
ready to leave off writing or, in the future, to
write only in order to defend the Faith of the

Church against the Calvinists. . . . But, if one comprises in it (the party) all those who entertain the same sentiments, and who doubt, no less than they, the fact in question, but who have found means to secure their own safety . . . then one may say with truthfulness that it is a very considerable one, and which comprises almost all the clever people in France, not only among the theologians, but also among the Bishops.'

It is a long letter, very eloquent, closely reasoned, and expressed with studied moderation, even when describing the injustice which had been done. In the accompanying missive to the Cardinal, Madame de Longueville adds that 'this conduct and these divisions' induce the real heretics to insult the Church, and to keep away those who would wish to return to the fold, and she finishes up with these words :

' It is true, Monsieur, that the compassion I feel for those poor women is the principal cause which has induced me to write to His Holiness on the subject, and which has also urged me to implore your Eminence to be their intercessor, assuring you that I shall feel infinitely obliged to you, and that there will be no occasion on which I shall not endeavour to prove my gratitude.'

The negotiations continued for a long time after the reception of these letters, which, however, produced a distinctly favourable impression. In the evening all those interested in the defence of. the victims of persecution met regularly at the Hôtel de Longueville, where they were eagerly expected and where the letters received from the Bishops and others were read and commented upon. By degrees some progress was made in Paris. Bargellini, the Papal Nuncio, was won over by the courtly grace of Gondrin. The great Arnauld, whose uncompromising attitude had been one of the main difficulties, became more moderate after having been for so long under the personal daily influence of Madame de Longueville. M. Pavillon, through his unyielding disposition as regarded the question of principle, was the obstacle that stood the longest in the way of a settlement. A compromise, suggested to the nuns in 1668, and urgently endorsed by the Duchess, failed. Even emigration came to be discussed as a way out of the dilemma. In 1667, however, a literary event took place which greatly helped to turn public opinion in favour of Port Royal. This was the famous translation of the New Testament, by MM. Le Maître, de Sacy, and Arnauld, known as *le Nouveau Testament de Mons*, which was revised at the Hôtel de Longueville. In its dainty garb it became not only the delight of theologians, but the fashionable religious book, thanks very largely to the great protectress of the translators, whose taste still gave the *ton*, in society, in all matters of this kind.

The attacks of the Jesuits, of course, increased its popularity, while making them somewhat ridiculous. Monsieur le Prince and all the Condé family were on the breach by this time, working for his sister's cause. All these things helped to prepare the way for that which was coming, namely, the great work of Madame de Longueville's life, the 'Peace of the Church.'

It became known that it was practically arranged to form a tribunal of Prelates to prosecute the four Bishops, and this had to be prevented at any price. At last the decision was come to by the little council of the party that a letter of respectful submission to the Pope should be indited and sent on behalf of the four Bishops, in which they would undertake to order, in their respective dioceses, that the 'Formulary' be signed, the right being reserved to each signatory to have a full explanation taken down in writing. This document, which was actually the work of Arnauld and Nicole, carried out under the eyes and in accordance with the advice of Madame de Longueville, was boldly signed by Gondrin on behalf of the Bishops, and on August 9, 1668, it was accepted by both parties. Great was the joy of the inmates of the Hôtel de Longueville. After sundry difficulties in obtaining the consent to what had been done of Bishop Pavillon, all was officially settled at last. The Nuncio had given his signature. The Pope's brief followed as a matter of course, and reached the King on October 8, 1668. In the same month Arnauld was presented to Louis XIV., accompanied by his nephew, M. de Pomponne, who was beginning to be a favourite

R

at Court.   Within a few days M. de Sacy, who
was still at the Bastille, received his liberty.
A great symbolical medal was struck, on
January 1, 1669, in honour of the ' Peace of
the Church.'   The King, the Nuncio and the
Ministers disavowed it, and it was ordered to be
defaced.   A strange symbol of what that peace
was destined to be.

In spite of all this the poor nuns were still
in their old sad plight, and Madame de Longueville could not rejoice fully in what had been
accomplished until that state of things should
have been remedied.   They held out longer
than any one else.   But at last they were persuaded to yield to the joint pleadings of
Arnauld and M. de Sacy, and to accept the
signature under the new conditions.

On February 18, the interdict was raised,
to the infinite joy of every one it concerned.
This was followed by the settlement of the
temporalities, in which a good deal of injustice
was done.   A separation took place between
the two Abbeys.   The Prince de Condé endeavoured to secure for the heroic recalcitrants

their Paris monastery by hinting to the Archbishop that his sister wished to retire to it
altogether, but in vain. The nuns who had
refused to sign the 'Formulary' were reduced to
their house of Port Royal des Champs, whilst
a dozen insignificant Sisters, under Mother
Dorothée Perdreau, were left in possession of
the Paris convent and of one half of the total
revenue of the two monasteries. From that
time the Paris house ceased to be, in any
characteristic sense, Port Royal. The last
representative of its former state was Madame
de Sablé. She remained in her home, undis-
turbed, till her death, assiduously and affectionately tended by the Duchess de Longueville.

The *Maison des Champs* had ten years of
peace and glory before it, in spite of fever and
poverty. Mother Agnès lived to enjoy it for
another two years. After her death Mother
Angélique de St. Jean became the soul of the
great convent. The boys' schools were never
reopened, a permanent loss to the growing
generation, but the girl boarders were more
numerous than ever. M. d'Andilly and

the remaining 'hermits' returned to their beloved 'desert' around the monastery.   Many distinguished persons built themselves houses within the charmed circle.   Mademoiselle de Vertus had hers, and eventually retired to the convent as a perpetual novice, which was as much as her health permitted her to do. Madame de Longueville built herself a house which by means of a gallery communicated with a tribune in the church, and in which she spent more and more of her time.

Pascal's 'Pensées' shed their glory over the autumn of Port Royal.

CHAPTER V

DECLINING YEARS AND DEATH

THE pacification of the Church which Madame de Longueville had so ardently desired was the real glory of her life. It was also the last public event in which she was directly concerned. Henceforth she lived more and more in retirement. M. Singlin had died in 1664, deeply mourned both by her and by Mademoiselle de Vertus, and when M. de Sacy, who succeeded him as their confessor, was imprisoned, he had to be replaced by M. Marcel, the Curé of St. Jacques du Haut Pas. He was in no sense the equal of these exceptional men, and does not seem to have been able to keep within bounds the excessive asceticism to which the Duchess naturally inclined.

To M. Singlin we owe a document which

is of the greatest interest to any student of Madame de Longueville's life, whilst one cannot help feeling that it was far too sacred for publication, even after the lapse of many years. One of the peculiarities of Port Royal was a habit of reducing everything to writing and preserving everything that had been written. Among so many virtues of the highest order there was wanting the small but important quality of good taste, which, indeed, was despised as unworthy to be taken into account by Christian men and women. Hence their archives disclose the most intimate recesses in the lives of individuals to an extent which shocks our feelings at every turn. The 'Self-examination' written by Madame de Longueville on November 24, 1661, by order of her new director, and immediately after her general confession to him, is, however, a most touching and interesting human document:[1]

'It is a long time since I began to seek (so it seemed to me) the way which leads to life, but I always thought I had not reached it without

---

[1] *Supplément au Nécrologe de Port-Royal,* in 4to, p. 137.

knowing exactly what was my obstacle. I felt
there was one between God and me, but I
knew it not, and I felt I was not really in my
place, and I was anxious to be there without
knowing where it was or how to look for it.   It
seems to me, on the other hand, since I have
placed myself under the direction of Monsieur
Singlin, that I am really in that place which I
sought for, that is, at the true entrance to the
path of Christian life, around which I had
wandered until now. . . .'

M. Singlin, who was a genuine searcher of
hearts, had placed his finger on the spot where
lay the true blemish of her life and character,
that pride and vanity which had once been the
mainspring of all her actions :

. . . 'The things which it (pride) produced
were not unknown to me, but I dwelt only
upon its effects, which, indeed, I considered
great imperfections ; still, by all that has now
been discovered to me, I can see I never went
to that source.   It is not that I was unaware
that pride had been the starting-point of all my
errors, but I did not believe it to be as living
as it is, and did not attribute to it all the wrongs
I committed, and yet I can see now that they
all originated there.   My soul was divided
between the love of pleasure and pride in the
days of my sinful life.   When I say pleasure I

mean intellectual pleasure, for others do not naturally attract me. Those two miserable motives have agreed so well together that during those miserable days they were the soul of my whole conduct. I therefore placed the pleasure which I so diligently strove after in what flattered my pride, and really in proposing to myself what the Demon proposed to our first parents—Ye shall be even as gods! And that saying which pierced their hearts has so lacerated mine that the blood still flows from that deep wound, and will long continue to flow unless Jesus Christ, by His grace, stops that effusion of blood.'

This discovery terrified her, and she speaks of being ' led to the verge of the temptation of discouragement.' It appears to her as if even her ' present docility ' were only her pride, ' which transforms itself, if one may say so, into an angel of light, in order to have something to live upon. . . .'

' On receiving the letter from M. Singlin, which it seemed to me must be a long one, and which thereby made me hope for much in that quarter which is what presently occupies me most, I opened it quickly, as my nature always prompts me to do when my mind is full of a subject ; whereas, on the contrary (I say this to make myself known as I am), it gives me such great negligence and coldness towards everything which does not occupy my mind, at the time, in a strong and exclusive manner. And that it is which causes some to think me violent and easily carried away, because they have seen me in my passions or even in my little inclinations and preferences, and others to think me slow and lazy, even dead, if one may use that word, because they have not seen me when I was moved with whatever has moved me for good or evil. That also is why I have been defined as if I were two different persons of opposite humours, which has caused it to be said, sometimes that I was double-faced, sometimes that my humour had changed, neither of which was true, but arose from the different situations in which they found me ; for I was dead as death to all that was not in my head, and all alive to the least particle of the things which touched me. I still have the same disposition, in a diminished form, and I allow it to govern me only too much. It is that disposition which caused me to open the letter quickly.'

She goes on to analyse her changeable humour and the occasional '*sècheresse*' and abruptness she displays towards people in her unguarded moments.

'Yet another thought about myself has come to me : it is that I am glad, from motives of vanity [*amour-propre*], that I should have been ordered to write this, because, above all things, I like to be occupied with myself and so to occupy others, and that vanity induces us to prefer to speak evil of ourselves rather than say nothing about ourselves.   I expose this thought also, and, while exposing it, I submit it like all the others. . . .'

Nothing could be more scrupulously truthful, more painstaking in its eager search after perfect accuracy, or more profoundly humble, than this long piece of self-analysis, and the reader feels that for once he is allowed to look into the innermost workings of one human being's consciousness.

This humility in one whose besetting sin had been pride is aptly illustrated by a small incident told by her contemporaries.   One day, when she was being carried in her chair from the Carmelites to the church of St. Jacques du Haut Pas, an officer to whom she had been obliged to refuse a favour of some kind insulted her in a loud voice, referring to the wicked libels La Rochefoucauld's 'Mémoires'

had spread abroad. Her servants were about
to fall upon him, when Madame de Longueville
called to them, 'Do him no harm! I have deserved far worse.' In the same spirit of Christian
forgiveness and self-humiliation, nothing would
induce her to allow Condé to punish Bussy-
Rabutin when he had slandered her in his
'Histoire Amoureuse des Gaules.'

A description of the Duchess, of which the
author is unknown, but which, in Sainte-Beuve's
opinion,[1] may have been by Nicole, shows her
as she appeared to an eye-witness since her
connection with Port Royal, when she was no
longer living in the world, yet not quite out '
of it :

'*Character of Madame de Longueville.*

'It was a thing to study the way in which
Madame de Longueville conversed with people.
Doing so afforded an opportunity of observing
those qualities which are equally estimable
according to the standard of God and that of
the world ; she never spoke ill of any one, and
she always showed she felt pained when one
spoke freely of the faults of others, even truthfully.

[1] A. C. Sainte-Beuve, *Protraits de Femmes.*

'She never said anything to her own advantage, that was so without exception.

'She seized, as much as she could do so without affectation, every opportunity of humbling herself.

'She said so well all that she said, that it would have been difficult to say it better however much one might have studied to do so.

'There were more lively and rare things in what M. de Tréville said, but there was more delicacy and as much wit and good sense in the way in which Madame de Longueville expressed herself.

'She spoke sensibly, modestly, charitably, and without passion.

'In her discourses one never noticed any bad reasoning.

'She listened a great deal, never interrupted, and showed no eagerness to speak.

'The air she liked least was the decisive, scientific air, and I know of some otherwise estimable persons whom she never appreciated because they had something of that air.

'It was on the contrary (*sic*) paying one's court to her to speak of every one with equity and without passion, and to esteem all the good there might be in each.

'In fine, her whole exterior, her voice, her face, her gestures, were a perfect music, and her mind and body served her so well to express whatever she desired to have understood that she was the most perfect actress in the world.'

One more Jansenist witness it may not be amiss to quote. M. de Pontchâteau, a 'hermit,' not given to flattery, wrote to his sister, the Duchesse d'Epernon, a few days after the death of the Protectress of Port Royal :

'Madame de Longueville has started for that long journey into eternity from which no one returns . . . and people will talk of nothing else for some time. . . . I believe her to be happy, and that God will have shown her His mercy. She greatly loved His Church and the poor, the two objects of our charity upon earth. . . .'

In his next letter he says :

'I do not like exaggeration, but it must be confessed that there was much that was extraordinary in the penance of Madame de Longueville, both as regards the body and the mind. . . . It is not that I wish to make out she was a saint who has gone to enjoy God immediately upon leaving this world . . . but it is true one will see few people of such quality embrace a life like hers, and abide firmly to the end in the great truths of religion, in a great contempt of herself, which was visible even in her attire, and in a uniformity, as regards her essential duties, such as she has always displayed. . . .'

Private troubles abounded during this last period of Madame de Longueville's life. Her two sons gave her little satisfaction. The eldest, the Comte de Dunois, was mentally below the average, and his whole existence was one of stupid dissipation. He had, nevertheless, taken orders, at the suggestion of the Prince de Condé and much against his mother's wishes and feelings, so that it was his younger brother, the Comte de St. Pol, who succeeded to his father's title, and became the last Duc de Longueville.[1] Finally, the eldest became a Jesuit, and the fact that he was countenanced by her brother in what she considered a sacrilege added bitterness to this trial. At last she was called to Normandy, whither she was accompanied by her faithful friend and almost constant companion, Mademoiselle de

[1] Châteaudun à Madame de Longueville, 23 et 27 juillet 1664. Madame de Longueville à Monsieur le Prince (2 letters), vol. 10586, fol. 1-7 (*Bibliothèque Nationale*).

Vertus, to ascertain that the unfortunate young man's mind was entirely shattered, and that he must be sequestrered from the world for the rest of his life.

The reception she met with on this occasion, in the province the reversion to the government of which her husband had secured for his two sons, shows the love and gratitude felt for her by the people. She describes it at the end of a letter to the Curé of St. Jacques du Haut Pas:

'My departure from Rouen was like my arrival. The people accompanied me as they had received me, blessing me, weeping, and showing all that the sincerest affection can express. M. Le Nain and Father Dubreuil were unable to restrain their tears. Nothing like the anxiety to see me was ever seen, and the space before my house, the steps and the rooms, were so full that it was impossible to go in or out. A remnant of worldly spirit made me take some pleasure in that.'[1]

Her relations to Condé did not suffer from the differences of opinion which had arisen between them respecting her eldest son. In a

[1] Bourgoing de Villefore, *La Véritable Vie*, etc.

letter of which the date is incomplete, but which was probably written at this time, Madame de Longueville tells him :

' I wish for it [his coming to live in the Faubourg St. Jacques] with all my heart, I assure you. I could not pay that compliment to many people, for, to speak the truth, there are very few left whose absence does not please me as well as their presence. Judge from that of the affection I have for you, and whether you are not bound to keep for me that which you have promised me.' [1]

The young Duc de Longueville, always her favourite son, was as gifted as the Comte de Dunois was the reverse. Such a good judge as Madame de La Fayette always spoke of him and his conversational powers in terms of the highest praise. The only letter of his that has been preserved is a little note to the Marquise d'Huxelles, who was on friendly terms with all the members of his family as well as with himself. In clearness and elegance of expression it is a generation in advance upon

[1] Madame de Longueville à Monsieur le Prince, le 5ᵉ octobre. MS. Fr. 12769, fol. 35 (*Bibliothèque Nationale*).

the involved and incorrect epistles of the time
of the Regency to which his mother and her
contemporaries belonged. The informal ' billet,'
or note, which had then recently come into
fashion, was said to have been 'invented' by
Madame de Sablé and the Comtesse de
Maure : [1]

[2] ' *September* 28.—You will believe me when
I say that I am no less pleased the King
should have given you all you had asked of him
than I was alarmed at the danger you ran of
having nothing. Every one is so convinced of
the interest I take in all that concerns you that
Monsieur de Romille desires me to convey his
compliments to you, believing, as he says, that
you will receive them more favourably coming
from me than from him. I acquit myself thereof,
and you will, if you please, bear witness to him
of the fact. I have no news of the Prince,
although I have written to him since he left.
Do what you can to induce him to give
me some. If you cannot obtain that much
let me know about him. They say we shall
leave here on the eleventh of next month.
Remember always, Madame la Marquise, the
best of your friends ; I should say the humblest

---

[1] *Histoire de la Princesse de Paphlagonie*, by ' Mademoiselle.'
[2] Vol. 12769, fol. 31 (unpublished), *Bibliothèque Nationale.*

of your servants, but that you permit such familiarity to me, at least in words.

'LE COMTE DE ST. POL.'

For some years he also led an irregular life. His mother felt it acutely, and it was therefore with intense satisfaction she saw him gradually give up the frivolous pursuits of his early youth and serve his country with distinction, under his uncle, in the war of 1667.

The great respect which was felt for Madame de Longueville by all, even her former enemies, extended to the King, who never missed an opportunity of showing it, in small matters as well as in greater ones,[1] in spite of her reluctance to come to court unless the strictest propriety required it of her.

Every anecdote in which Louis XIV. had a part was considered supremely important, and so it is duly recorded, by Villefore, how one day, when she came to see the Duchesse de Richelieu at Versailles, and did not find her

---

[1] Madame de Longueville au Roy, 22 juin 1668 (*Bibliothèque Nationale*).

at home, she was seen by her brother from a
window in the King's room.

'Here is my sister,' he said, 'who will have
to dine at the inn, because her friend is away.'

'She will not dine at the inn ; she will dine
with me,' said the King.

It was an odd situation in the light of a not
very distant past.

Another story is better worth telling. With
something of her old impulsiveness, Madame de
Longueville had indulged in rather strong
criticism of her royal cousin, *à propos* of a question connected with Port Royal, in the hearing
of a person who repeated it. Louis XIV.
asked Monsieur le Prince whether she had
really used the expressions attributed to her.
He vowed and declared it was impossible.
'I will believe it if she says so,' replied the
King. Condé went to his sister and argued
with her for hours, imploring her to deny that
she had made the speech complained of, but
nothing would induce her to exonerate herself
by a lie. She went straight to the monarch,
and, throwing herself at his feet, told him the

simple truth, and begged his forgiveness. From
that time he showed her greater confidence and
consideration than ever before. Those whom
she had taken under her protection benefited
by this genuine esteem, but only as long as she
lived.

In 1672 there came upon her the crushing
grief of her declining years. Her favourite
son was killed during the passage of the Rhine,
where, with the impetuosity which was in the
Condé blood, he had pressed forward, almost
alone. The whole story has been told by
Madame de Sévigné, and must not be retold in
other words than hers:

[1] 'Paris, Friday, June 17 (1672) at eleven in the evening.

'As soon as I had sent off my packet, I
heard, my dear, a sad news, of which I shall
not tell you the details, because I do not know
them ; but I do know that during the passage
of the Yssel, under the command of Monsieur
le Prince, Monsieur de Longueville was killed.
The news is crushing. . . . Ever so many have
perished on this occasion. . . . M. le Prince
was wounded in the hand. M. de Longueville

[1] *Lettres de Madame de Sévigne.*

had forced the barrier, which he had reached
first, and he was also killed first. . . . All the
rest is in keeping. . . . But at last the Yssel
has been passed. M. le Prince crossed three
or four times in a boat quite quietly, giving his
orders everywhere with that coolness and that
divine valour which you know. It is stated
that, after those first difficulties, no more
enemies are to be seen.'

‘ Paris, June 20 (1672).

‘. . . The state of Madame de Longueville is
heartrending, they say. I have not seen her,
but this is what I know. Mademoiselle de Vertus
had returned to Port Royal, where she spends
most of her time. They went to fetch her, with
Monsieur Arnauld, to impart the terrible news.
It was sufficient for her to show herself: so sudden
a return pointed to something fatal. Indeed,
as soon as she appeared, “ Ah, Mademoiselle,
how is my brother ? ” Her thoughts dared go no
further. “ Madame, his wound is doing well.”
“ Then there has been a fight ? And my
son ? ” She received no answer. “ Ah, Mademoiselle, my son, my dear child ; answer me,
is he dead ? ” “ Madame, I have no words to
answer you.” “ Ah, my dear son, did he die
on the spot ? Had he not a single moment ?
Ah, my God, what a sacrifice ! ” and thereupon
she falls on her bed, and all that the sharpest
grief can do, convulsions and fainting fits, and
mortal silence and stifled cries, and bitter tears,

impulses to Heaven, and tender pitiable lamentations—she went through everything. She sees certain people, she takes some broth, because it is the will of God. She has no rest. Her health, already so bad, is visibly affected. As for me I wish she may die, not being able to understand how she can live after such a loss.'

She did live, for seven more years, because it was the will of God, sustained in this her greatest trial by the knowledge she afterwards obtained that, on the day of his death and before starting for battle, her son had made a general confession and given proofs of Christian and charitable sentiments, which was the only consolation his mother was still capable of feeling. Madame de Sévigné wrote once more to her daughter, on June 27 :

'At last I have seen Madame de Longueville. Chance placed me near her bed. She made me come closer to her still, and spoke to me first, for, as for me, I know no words at such a moment. She told me that she did not doubt I pitied her ; that nothing was wanting in her misfortune. She spoke of Madame de La Fayette and Monsieur d'Hacqueville as of those who would feel most compassion for her ;

she spoke to me of my son and of the friendship her son had felt for him. I do not tell you what were my answers.'

Six months before that crowning grief, Madame de Longueville had lost her favourite sister-in-law, the Princess de Conti. The Prince had predeceased her on February 21, 1666, after a genuine and consistent 'conversion,' which induced him also to spend the last few years of his life in endeavours to undo the harm he had done. He made restitution on a large scale, both to those who had been ruined by the Fronde and to the Church, whose privileges and benefices he had too long enjoyed and misused. His wife had likewise become 'converted' in a different sense, for her life had been a blameless one. She had become an ardent follower of Port Royal, and Madame de Sévigné had christened her and Madame de Longueville the 'Mothers of the Church.'

Madame de Sablé died fifteen months before her friend, and Mademoiselle de Vertus had finally retired to Port Royal des Champs, so that the loneliness of the evening of life closed in more and more on her whose career had once been so sunny and so brilliant. She longed for the complete seclusion and peace of the cloister, but there was work to be done still, and she felt that it was necessary for the protection of her Jansenist friends that she should not altogether retire from the world.

After the tragic death of her son the Duchess left the Hôtel de Longueville, in which she never lived again. She withdrew to the retreat she had secured for herself in the valley of Chevreuse, close to Port Royal. Henceforth she divided her time between this home and her lodging at the Carmelites. She was there when Mademoiselle de La Vallière took her vows, and was a much-moved spectator at that touching ceremony. She also witnessed the arrival of the heart of the great Turenne, over which she had once reigned supreme. Years afterwards, Madame d'Humières, a friend and correspondent of Madame de Sablé,[1] who was the next occupant of her rooms at the 'Great

---

[1] Madame d'Humières à la Marquise de Sablé, 10591, fol. 29 (*Bibliothèque Nationale*).

Convent,' used to point to the floor of her
apartment and say, ' This is where Madame de
Longueville slept on the bare ground, for in
those days there were no boards.'

All these austerities, and a mind which
throughout her long penance had never been
quite at rest, had worn out her naturally delicate frame.

Only about a month before her death, we
are told, she entered into that perfect peace and
confidence for which she had longed so ardently.
She died at the convent of the Carmelites on
April 15, 1679, in her sixtieth year, revered by
all who knew her. By her bedside was the
brother who had been her earliest affection.
Of all those she had loved, he alone was left.

In accordance with her own directions,
her body was deposited in the church of the
Carmelites and her heart at Port Royal. Her
funeral oration was pronounced by La Roquette.
the insignificant Bishop of Autun, instead of
by Bossuet, who performed that duty towards
Condé.

Monsieur le Prince, who had asked that he

should do so for the Princess Palatine, did not venture to make the same request for his sister. The great divine could not have said of her as he did of Anne de Gonzague : ' In the famous questions which have troubled in so many ways the peace of our days she loudly declared that it was not for her to take any other part than that of obedience to the Church.'

Posterity thereby lost a masterpiece, for, with such a subject, it could not have been anything else, and the advantage of a portrait of Madame de Longueville, complete in itself, grand and harmonious in treatment, as were all those the immortal preacher has given us.

The picturesque elements which go to make up the history of her chequered career are singularly striking ; still more so a certain symmetry, a curious balance in the leading events of her life. She was born in the dungeon of Vincennes, near which, two hundred years later, the last Prince of her House was killed.[1] She ended her days in the very house

---

[1] The Duc d'Enghien, shot by order of Napoleon I. on March 28, 1804.

of prayer in which she had so longed to live. After sowing strife and causing war, it was given to her to deserve the beatitude promised to peace-makers.

Anne-Geneviève de Bourbon had not been dead three weeks before the persecutions against the Jansenists broke out afresh. As long as she lived the King had been restrained by his great personal respect for her. He did not hesitate for a moment as soon as she was gone. Louis XIV. disliked a body without a head, a little spiritual kingdom within his own which attracted an undue amount of attention. The monastery itself continued for some years to be regarded with admiration and reverence, but its days were numbered. Arnauld died in exile. The final dispersion came at last. The Peace of the Church did not survive Madame de Longueville, and thus the death in retirement of the self-effaced and humble penitent who, for years, had striven only for justice and concord meant bitter strife and proved a public calamity.

APPENDIX

BIOGRAPHICAL NOTES

NOTE A, page 67.

Maréchal d'Ancre (Concino Concini). Accompanied Marie de Médicis to France, on her marriage in 1600, and with his wife rose to the highest favour. Became Prime Minister to Louis XIII., who, at the instigation of the nobles by whom the marshal was hated, consented to his assassination in 1617.

NOTE B, page 13.

Anne of Austria, daughter of Philip III., King of Spain. Was born in 1602. Married Louis XIII. in 1615. Became Regent in 1643. Died 1666.

NOTE C, page 65.

Marquis de Châteauneuf (Charles de l'Aubespine). Was made Keeper of the Seals by Richelieu in 1630, but suspected of being a creature of Madame de Chevreuse and arrested in 1633. Remained in prison till the death of Louis XIII. Anne of Austria restored the seals to him.

He was exiled two years later and joined the Fronde. After he had been taken into favour again, was made Prime Minister in Mazarin's absence. Died 1653.

NOTE D, page 51.

Duchesse de Chevreuse (Marie de Rohan-Montbazon). Born 1600. Married, in 1617, Charles d'Albert, Duc de Luynes, Constable of France, and, in 1622, Charles de Lorraine, Duc de Chevreuse. Was a favourite of Queen Anne of Austria, and as such was persecuted and exiled by Richelieu. Was afterwards alienated from the queen. Negotiated both with Spain and Mazarin during the Fronde. Returned to court during the second part of the Fronde. Died 1679.

NOTE E, page 51.

Marquis de Cinq-Mars (H. Coiffier de Ruzé). Styled 'Monsieur le Grand' because he was 'Grand Ecuyer de France.' Born 1620. Conspired against his first protector, Cardinal Richelieu, and drew Gaston, Duc d'Orléans, into a plot, in the course of which he made a treaty with Spain. Was arrested, together with De Thou, at Narbonne, betrayed by Gaston, and executed at the same time as De Thou, at Lyons, in 1642.

NOTE F, page 14.

Gaston, Duke of Orleans, 'Monsieur,' son of Henri IV. and Marie de Médicis and brother of Louis XIII.

Born 1608. Married, first, the heiress of the Montpensiers and, after her death, secretly, Marguerite de Lorraine. Took a leading part in the various plots against Cardinal Richelieu, invariably betraying friends and fellow conspirators to save himself. Became Lieutenant-General of the Kingdom at the death of Louis XIII. Was a patron of arts and letters. Died 1660.

NOTE G, page 28.

Mazarin (Giulio). Born at Pescina in 1602. Became a soldier. Was employed on diplomatic missions by the Roman Curia, and, in 1631, brought about the peace of Cherasco. Entered the Church in 1632. Having been appointed Legate Extraordinary of the Holy See to Paris, attracted the attention of Richelieu, who caused him to be naturalised in 1639, and made a Cardinal in 1641. He recommended him to Louis XIII. as his successor when on his death-bed, and the King appointed him member of the Council of Regency.

NOTE H, page 64.

Molé (Mathieu), son of a distinguished magistrate. Born 1584. Became Procureur-Général in 1614, First President of the Parliament of Paris in 1641, Keeper of the Seals in 1650. Resigned the latter office in order to facilitate the reconciliation of the opposite parties in the State. Was persuaded to resume it and retained the seals till his death in 1656. Left valuable memoirs.

NOTE I, page 31.

The Princess Palatine (Anne de Gonzague), daughter of the Duc de Nevers. Born 1616. Married Prince Edward, 'Count Palatine,' son of the Elector Palatine Frederick V. Died 1684.

NOTE J, page 241.

Marquis de Pomponne (Simon Arnauld), son of M. d'Andilly, and nephew of 'le Grand Arnauld.' Born 1618. Was Foreign Minister under Louis XIV. Died 1699. Left memoirs.

NOTE K, page 46.

Vicomte de Turenne (Henri de la Tour d'Auvergne), son of the Duc de Bouillon. Born 1611. Made Marshal of France in 1643. Commanded the Army of the Rhine. Joined the Fronde in 1659. Afterwards hastened the conclusion of the Treaty of the Pyrenees by his victories. He was originally a Huguenot, but was converted to Catholicism by Bossuet. Killed at Salzbach, July 27, 1675.

INDEX

T.

PRINTED BY
SPOTTISWOODE AND CO., NEW-STREET SQUARE
LONDON

www.ingramcontent.com/pod-product-compliance
Lightning Source LLC
Chambersburg PA
CBHW060605030726
47498CB00005B/1556